Prairie Brides: Book Two

**Other Prairie Brides Series Books
in Large Print:**

Prairie Brides: Book One
The Bride's Song by Linda Ford
The Barefoot Bride by Linda Goodnight

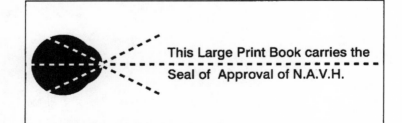

This Large Print Book carries the
Seal of Approval of N.A.V.H.

Prairie Brides:

Book Two

A Homesteader, a Bride and a Baby
JoAnn A. Grote

A Vow Unbroken
Amy Rognlie

Thorndike Press • Waterville, Maine

Published in 2005 by arrangement with Barbour Publishing, Inc.

Thorndike Press® Large Print Christian Fiction.

The tree indicium is a trademark of Thorndike Press.

The text of this Large Print edition is unabridged.
Other aspects of the book may vary from the original edition.

Set in 16 pt. Plantin by Liana M. Walker.

Printed in the United States on permanent paper.

Library of Congress Cataloging-in-Publication Data

    Prairie brides : Book two / by JoAnn A. Grote [and] Amy Rognlie.
       p. cm. — (Thorndike Press large print Christian fiction)
    ISBN 0-7862-7979-6 (lg. print : hc : alk. paper)
    1. Love stories, American. 2. Women pioneers — Fiction. 3. Widows — Fiction. 4. Frontier and pioneer life — Fiction. 5. Historical fiction, American. 6. Large type books. I. Grote, JoAnn A. Homesteader, a bride and a baby. II. Rognlie, Amy. Vow unbroken. III. Series. IV. Thorndike Press large print Christian fiction series.
    PS648.L6P7253 2005
    813´.08508358—dc22
                                          2005015638

Dedicated to
my grandniece and grandnephew,
Alexis Olsen and Brett Olsen
who are descended
from Minnesota pioneers

As the Founder/CEO of NAVH, the only national health agency solely devoted to those who, although not totally blind, have an eye disease which could lead to serious visual impairment, I am pleased to recognize Thorndike Press* as one of the leading publishers in the large print field.

Founded in 1954 in San Francisco to prepare large print textbooks for partially seeing children, NAVH became the pioneer and standard setting agency in the preparation of large type.

Today, those publishers who meet our standards carry the prestigious "Seal of Approval" indicating high quality large print. We are delighted that Thorndike Press is one of the publishers whose titles meet these standards. We are also pleased to recognize the significant contribution Thorndike Press is making in this important and growing field.

Lorraine H. Marchi, L.H.D.
Founder/CEO
NAVH

* Thorndike Press encompasses the following imprints: Thorndike, Wheeler, Walker and Large Print Press.

A Homesteader,
a Bride and a Baby

by JoAnn A. Grote

Chapter 1

Minnesota prairie, 1878

"I didn't even have a chance to say good-bye."

The prairie wind snatched away the whispered words as soon as they left Lorette Taber's lips. The ever-present breeze swept through the tall prairie grasses that surrounded the four fresh graves, as though asking, "Why are their deaths more important than those of the thousands of other creatures I've seen die in this land?"

The wind whipped waving strands of prairie grass around the simple wooden crosses that stood at the heads of the graves. *Already reclaiming Bess and Tom and swallowing up their dreams for this place,* Lorette thought.

The earthy smell of freshly turned graves and wild grasses, the rough untamed land beneath her feet, the forlorn whistle of unceasing wind, all joined in concert to punctuate nature's power and man's helplessness in attempting to conquer these lands.

Viney stems of tiny pale pink wild roses were wrapped about each cross. The meaning of their presence came through the fog of Lorette's loss and pain. Someone else missed her sister and family.

The child in her arms stirred, rubbing his eyes against the shoulder of her once-crisp blue traveling suit. He uttered tentative cries, pausing briefly between each, waiting to see whether the comforting presence of the parents for whom he longed would be given before he began crying in earnest.

Lorette's heart crimped. She rubbed one hand lightly over the nine-month-old baby's back, pressed her cheek gently against his soft, short baby hair, and murmured, "Poor Samuel. Your mommy and daddy still love you. They'll always love you. You'll never be alone, I promise. I'll always be with you."

Her eyes blurred. Could Samuel comprehend that he'd never see his parents and older brother and sister in this world again? Of course he was too young to understand their deaths in terms of logic and words, but did his infant spirit sense his loss in some mysterious way known only to God? Over the last twenty-four hours, had he felt abandoned by the four people who had cared for him all of his short life?

"Miss Taber?"

At the sound of a man's deep voice, she swung around, pulling Samuel protectively closer. She didn't answer, only stared at the blond man whose steady gray gaze met hers.

The wind didn't blow away the powerful odor of dirt, sweat, and kerosene emanating from him. He wore the flour sack shirt and heavy denim trousers of a farmer. A wide soft-brimmed hat, a sweat ring about the crown, hung from one hand.

"I'm Chase Lankford, your sister's neighbor. I helped out on their farm some."

A bit of tension left her muscles at his gentlemanly manner and the knowledge of his name. "Bess mentioned you in her letters. She said you were a good friend to her and her husband."

He nodded once, briskly. "Yes, miss.

They were good people. I'm sorry for your loss."

Samuel pushed himself away from Lorette with his tiny fists, then with pudgy arms outstretched leaned toward Chase. "Uh. Uh."

His sudden, unexpected movement threw Lorette out of balance. She leaned with him, attempting to adjust her hold.

Chase grabbed him. "Careful there, big boy."

Lorette caught her breath as she watched him swing the baby to his side. She started to reach for Samuel, hesitated, then let her hands drop to her sides. Chase looked comfortable with the child, she realized, as though he'd held Samuel many times.

Watching them, Lorette pushed from her blue eyes a strand of black hair, which the wind had tugged from the thick figure eight at the back of her head. She thought it a wonder the wind hadn't blown off her dainty traveling hat.

Chase lifted Samuel until their eyes were on the same level and grinned. Samuel grinned back. Giggling, he touched his round little fingers to Chase's unshaven cheeks.

Lorette smiled. Obviously Samuel and Chase were friends, the boy happy with someone he knew. Her heart ached with the thought that Chase might be the only person left whom Samuel truly knew.

She turned back to the graves, blinking away tears. "It's so hard to believe they are gone. I got off the train expecting them to meet me. Instead I was met by a woman I didn't know who told me they were dead and handed over Samuel." She spoke painfully around the lump that had formed in her throat. "Diphtheria, she said."

Lorette was aware he stepped up beside her, that he swallowed as though he had a lump in his own throat. "Yes, diphtheria."

"It was so sudden. How could it happen so fast?"

"At first they thought they only had sore throats. When Bess and Tom realized that their sickness was more serious, Tom went after the doctor. Doc was miles out in the country on the other side of town on a call. By the time Tom found him, Tom was so weak himself from the diphtheria that Doc insisted he stay where he was while Doc came here. He was too late. Aaron and Liza, Bess and Tom's oldest children, were already dead. Bess died within hours. Tom never made it home again. He died at the farmhouse where he found Doc."

"Samuel never took the disease?"

"Hasn't shown any signs of it. Doc thinks the others caught it through contaminated milk, and Sam wouldn't have had any, him being . . ." Chase's tan took on a dusky tint.

Him being still at his mother's breast, Lorette completed silently, feeling her own cheeks heat.

"Bess had her hands full taking care of herself and the sick children," Chase continued, "so Kari Bresven offered to care for Sam until they were better."

"She was the one who met me at the railway station."

"Yes."

"Why couldn't the funeral have waited until I arrived? They only died yesterday."

"The bodies had to be buried right away to keep others from getting sick."

"I didn't even get to say good-bye." Her voice broke. Sobs welled up inside her, forcing their way through her chest and throat. She pressed a hand to her mouth, desperate to hold back what she feared would be a flood. A shaky gasp escaped.

A curious frown drew Samuel's blond eyebrows together. The fingers that had been playing with the top button of Chase's shirt stopped, and Samuel stared at her. She turned away, not wanting the

14

boy to see her break down. "P–please, may I have a few minutes alone?" The strangled sobs mixed with her words, and she wasn't sure Chase could understand her.

She was relieved when he said, "Sure. Sam and I will be waiting in the yard."

Soft swishing sounds told her Chase was walking away through the tall grass. Lorette sank to the ground beside the black dirt covering her sister's grave. "Oooh, Bess!" Realization of her loss cramped her stomach. She wrapped her arms about her middle, bent into the pain, and let her sobs flow onto the prairie winds.

Lorette hesitated at the yard's edge and surveyed the house. The two-story white frame building was simple in design. It looked like many others she'd seen in the nearby town and passed in the country on the way here. A porch ran across half the front of the house. The paint looked new, glistening merrily in the sunlight. Lilac bushes, past their blossoming season, waved near the corner of the porch. What Chase had referred to as a yard was swept dirt and poorly cropped prairie grass.

Chase and Samuel sat beside the well. It was topped by a twirling windmill that made Lorette think of a misshapen steeple. She could hear Samuel's baby laugh as a black and brown dog with a waggling tail poked its nose into Samuel's face. Chase grinned down at the two. Lorette smiled at the sweet picture they made. Then her eyes misted. No one looking at this cheerful home and the man, baby, and dog would suspect the life-and-death struggle that had so recently transpired here.

She took a deep, shaky breath and started toward Chase and Samuel. A strong odor caused her to wrinkle her nose. What was it? Nothing that smelled like any farm she'd ever been on.

Chase looked up as she neared. The gray eyes set in a spray of wrinkles were laughing. She assumed the wrinkles came from years of squinting against the sun. He nodded at the dog. "Meet Curly. He and Sam are great friends."

She smiled in return. "I can see that."

Samuel buried his head in Curly's fur and rubbed his face back and forth, a funny little baby growl in his throat. Curly just wiggled. Chase and Lorette laughed together at the sight.

Chase stood. Without his support, Samuel tipped from his sitting position to his side in the grass. Curly stuck his nose

16

in Samuel's stomach, instigating a delighted giggle.

Chase reached for a dipper tied to the well, dipped it into the wooden bucket, and handed it to Lorette.

"Thank you," she murmured. The cool water felt good. It tasted more metallic than the water back in Philadelphia. She handed the emptied dipper back to him. "I'd like to see the inside of the house."

"That's not possible."

His quick response startled her. She drew herself up, squaring her shoulders beneath her wilted traveling jacket. "You might recall that I am Bess's sister." She whirled about and started toward the house.

"Lorette! Miss Taber!"

She ignored him. A moment later she felt his large hand on her shoulder. She kept walking, and the hand slid away. Chase fell into place beside her, with Samuel caught securely about the middle in one strong arm.

"I apologize, Miss Taber. I'm not trying to order you about, but the house is being disinfected."

She stopped short. "What?"

"Doc said it had to be disinfected with sulfur smudges. After everything was

17

washed down, that is. You'll barely be able to breathe if you go inside now. It needs to be aired out."

"Oh." So that was the strange odor she'd smelled, sulfur. She felt ashamed for her hasty conclusion that he considered himself in a position to tell her what she could and could not do. Lorette tipped her head to one side, studying Chase's earnest face. "Are you saying you did this yourself, disinfecting the house?"

"Well, yes." He shifted Samuel's position. "I hope you don't feel I was invading your family's privacy. I didn't think you should have to clean up after . . . everything. . . ." His usually strong voice tapered off.

Lorette could think of nothing to say. This stranger had taken upon himself the task of cleaning up after the death of his good friends in order to spare someone he didn't know the unpleasant experience. Surely such a chore had been difficult for him. "Thank you." Her gratitude hoarsened her voice on the inadequate words. "The crosses . . . did you make them, too?"

"Yes. You'll want to replace them, I'm sure, but it didn't seem right, nothing marking the graves."

No wonder there were deep gray circles beneath his eyes. He must have been up all night taking care of things that would normally have fallen upon her shoulders. "And the wild roses on the graves?"

"Mrs. Bresven brought them. They grow wild on the prairie. Neighboring farmers dug the graves, and their families came for the service, those who weren't sick themselves. Bess and Tom were special people. Everyone liked them."

A cloud of helplessness enveloped Lorette. The house with its sulfur fumes was not available to her. There was nothing more she could do at the graves.

Chase cleared his throat. "What are you planning to do now?"

She tried to focus her thoughts. "Bess arranged a position for me as a governess with a family in town."

"The Henrys. She told me."

"I suppose I should speak with them next. I'm not certain they will welcome another child in their home." Her gaze shifted to Samuel, who was beginning to struggle in Chase's arms, impatient for release and new experiences.

"I'm sure the Henrys will understand if you take a day or two to get your bearings first, all things considered. The Bresvens would welcome you at their place for a few days, until you get things straight in your mind."

She remembered Kari Bresven, the plump, middle-aged Scandinavian woman who had met her at the station, had extended that offer when she drove them out to the farm in the Bresvens' buckboard, but Lorette had been too much in shock to register her need at that time. "I couldn't impose on strangers. Isn't there a hotel or boardinghouse in town?"

"Yes, miss, but I think you and the boy would be more comfortable at the Bresvens', if you don't mind my saying so. No one's a stranger to Mrs. Bresven. She likes having children around. She must. She has a passel of her own."

Lorette brushed the back of her hand across her forehead, noting with mild surprise that her skin was not only sweaty but also gritty from the dust blown about by the wind. She felt weary to her bones. She shouldn't accept a neighbor's hospitality when there was a hotel in town, but the town suddenly seemed a continent away. "If you're certain Mrs. Bresven won't mind —"

Bouncing on the hard seat of a buckboard beside Chase Lankford on the short ride to the Bresven farm, Lorette ran quickly through possibilities for her immediate future. They appeared dismally few in number. If the Henrys would not take her on because of Samuel, what would she do? She no longer had a position to return to in Philadelphia. The family for whom she'd worked there had already hired a new governess. Finding another position anywhere would be difficult. Parents who hired a governess usually wanted all the governess's attention given to their own children.

Lorette drew the boy in her lap into a quick hug. Abandoning him to strangers wasn't to be considered. He was the only family she had now, and she was his only family. They needed to stick together.

Standing beside the rough driveway on the Bresven farm, Lorette watched Chase drive away on the clattering buckboard, dust rising in small clouds from beneath the wooden and metal wheels. Samuel whimpered in her arms, already missing Chase.

"It's all right, Samuel," she whispered in his ear. "I'm not going anywhere. It's you and me now."

The Lord always makes a way.

The words she'd heard her mother re-
peat hundreds of times spoke softly in her
mind. Lorette's gaze swept the prairie. In
the distance she could see Bess and Tom's
house. A couple other farmhouses stood
on the horizon. There were no trees, only
fields, and a seemingly endless ocean of
undulating prairie grass, amongst which
Chase and the buckboard and the dust
clouds were already lost to her view.

Could the Lord make a way for her and
Samuel even in such a place as this?

The wagon jolted along over the road
that was barely more than two deep ruts in
a prairie that had been unbroken and untamed ten years ago. Chase felt as jolted
emotionally as he did physically, bouncing
along on the leather cushioned seat.

He'd been working without sleep since
he'd discovered the deaths of his friends.
He closed his mind now as he had again
and again to the horror of discovering Bess
and the children and hearing the story of
Tom's desperate and futile search for the
doctor before Tom succumbed to the disease himself. Helping with the graves,
putting together the makeshift crosses with
shaking hands, disinfecting the home —
he'd worked through it all grateful to have

someplace to put his energy, grateful for the reprieve from the depths of grief he knew were to come.

He was teetering on the edge of grief's abyss now, he knew. He recognized the place and dreaded it.

It was the realization that Sam, the last living part of Tom and Bess, might soon also leave his life that brought him to the edge. The hardest thing ever required of him was to ride away leaving that little boy in a stranger's arms, even though that stranger was Bess's sister. Even though he knew from everything Bess had told him of Lorette that Bess would completely trust Sam to her sister's care.

Chase didn't trust anyone but himself to care for that boy. Lorette hadn't even laid eyes on Sam until a couple hours ago. How could she possibly care for the boy as much as Chase cared?

He wished it were possible to keep the boy from missing his parents. He wished he could bring him up with laughter and love and a respect for the land and hard work and faith in God, the way Tom and Bess would have raised him. He wished. . . .

"I just want to protect him," he whispered fiercely.

There was no reply to the words, which had been a prayer. Only the insects that dwelt in the prairie grass and cornfields spoke, creating the incessant music of the homesteaders' rolling land.

He hadn't been able to protect Tom and Bess and the kids from diphtheria. Now he couldn't protect their son from grief or from anything else. He had no right. It was Lorette who would decide Sam's future.

The pain that had been building inside him burst. The tears he hadn't had time to shed flowed down his cheeks.

Chase flicked the reins, urging the horses into a canter. He longed to escape the pain that engulfed him. He wanted to run. But he knew that there was no hiding place from this sorrow.

Chapter 2

Lorette sat beside Mrs. Henry in church, the service going by in a daze. She sang the hymns and responded with the rest of the congregation to the readings without comprehending the words. Her only communication with God was the constant cry in her heart and mind, *What now, Lord? Help us!*

Mrs. Henry had drawn her aside right before they left for church. The scene replayed through her mind. It had started with a compliment. "You are wonderful with our children," Mrs. Henry had said. "The two weeks you've been with us have proven that. There's no question of your ability or dedication, but we hired a governess because we want our children to have that person's undivided attention.

You must admit that with Samuel here, you are unable to give my children your first duty. Mr. Henry and I would like you to stay on as governess, but it will only be possible if you find another home for Samuel."

Lorette's fear for her and Samuel's futures swirled through her. On her meager salary, could she possibly afford to pay someone to care for Samuel while she was at work each day? Not likely.

When the service was over she followed the rest of the congregation outside into the early summer sunshine. All around her people chatted in friendly groups, but she knew only the Henrys.

"Good morning, Miss Taber."

She blinked in surprise at the masculine voice and looked up at the tall man beside her. He looked familiar, but she couldn't place him. Samuel, who had been watching the crowd from the safety of her arms, lunged for the man. Lorette gasped and leaned with the boy.

"Whoa, there, fella." The man grinned as he effortlessly lifted Samuel from Lorette's arms.

"Why, Mr. Lankford, I didn't recognize you." Lorette pressed gloved fingers to her lace-covered throat, realizing too late that he might take her comment for an insult. The man wasn't covered with sweat and dust today. He was dressed in a simple brown suit and was as clean and close-shaven as any of the other men in church.

"There's a number of churches out near the farm site, but their services are in Norwegian or Swedish or German due to the immigrant settlers. I try to make it into town for services whenever I can."

Lorette relaxed slightly. She rather liked it that this young man would make the uncomfortable trip to church without prodding from a mother or sister or wife.

Samuel bent forward and put his lips about the brim of Lankford's hat. "Samuel, don't." She tried to pry the brim from Samuel's busy mouth and tight grip.

"That's all right, miss. It's an old hat."

Lorette tried not to cringe, realizing it was the same sweat-stained hat the man had worn the day they met, though it looked as though the worst of the dust had been knocked from it. She gave Mr. Lankford a wavering smile and continued with her attempts to release the hat. "Just the same, it's best he not try to eat it."

Lankford cleared his throat. "I was wondering if you'd like to see your sister's house. I've been airing it out and the sulfur smell's gone now. Well, mostly gone. I thought perhaps you'd have the afternoon free, since it's Sunday and all." He nodded toward the dirt road where a couple dozen buggies, carriages, and wagons were lined up behind tethered horses. "I brought the wagon and would be glad to drive you out to the farm."

The fog of confusion that had hung about her since Mrs. Henry's announcement lifted momentarily. What a welcome break it would be to have a couple hours away from the Henry home and the talk she must eventually have with Mrs. Henry. "Thank you, Mr. Lankford. That would be lovely."

The smell of sulfur still lingered strong in the home when Lorette stepped over the threshold in spite of Mr. Lankford's assurances. Her nose wrinkled in reaction to the spoiled-egg odor. Samuel squeezed his eyes shut and screwed up his face in distaste. Lorette and Chase burst into laughter, and the protective shell of fear and grief that had encased Lorette's heart began to crack.

Sunshine poured through white curtains with blue and yellow embroidered flowers, cheering the large, high-ceilinged kitchen.

Blue and white dishes brightened an open cupboard along one wall. The nickel plating on the combination cooking and heating stove glistened as if polished yesterday. A cast-iron teakettle sat atop the stove ready for use.

Lorette ran a gloved fingertip lightly across the top of the rectangular wooden table where the family had shared meals. Except for a kerosene lamp, which needed cleaning, the table stood empty. It was as if the room waited for Bess to enter again and bustle about caring for her family. "Bess was so excited about this house."

"So was Tom."

Chase's words startled her. She hadn't realized she'd spoken aloud.

"Bess and Tom spent a winter planning this house," Chase continued. "When the snow is covering the ground for months, a farmer has time to make repairs and plan for spring. Every time I'd stop over that winter Tom and Bess were seated at this very table in their soddy pouring over their sketches of this house, arguing good-naturedly over the size of rooms and where to try and save money."

Lorette shook her head. "I could never imagine my sister living in a sod house."

"She never complained." Chase swung a

hand casually toward a window through which Lorette could see the barn. "They turned the house into a barn after they moved in here."

Lorette felt her cheeks blanch, not only appalled that her sister had lived in a dirt home but one that had become a home for farm animals. Yet Bess's letters had always been filled with plans and hopes and dreams and the excitement of her life with Tom in this land.

Chase indicated a doorway with his hat. "Sitting room's this way."

Lorette moved to the doorway and stopped, surveying the second of the two first-floor rooms. Just as Bess's kitchen took the place of both kitchen and dining room, the "sitting room," as Chase called it, combined both parlor and family room. She knew Bess had hoped to eventually add on a parlor and dining room.

Blushing tan roses on a rich brown background papered the walls. Maroon velvet draperies framed the tall windows. In the center of the room stood a large round table of dark wood, a kerosene lamp with a painted glass shade in the exact middle of the table's marble top. A gentlemen's chair, an armless ladies' chair and camel-back sofa, all framed in intricate carving and upholstered in plush fabric which matched the draperies, were set about the room with small marble-topped tables beside them. Dainty, snowy white crocheted pieces protected the furniture from hair oils.

"I remember how proud Bess was when she wrote of buying this furniture," Lorette said.

A bittersweet sadness twisted inside her. Everything in the room shouted its newness. To Lorette, the room seemed a pitiful attempt to capture the beauty of a parlor from back East, an impossible task in a four-room house on the prairie.

Samuel was poking with a pudgy finger at the watch which hung from a silver breast pin on Lorette's green swirled gingham dress. After a moment of observation, he flopped his head forward and tried to put the watch in his mouth.

"No, Samuel." Lorette pried the strong little wet fingers from his mouth and the watch from his fingers, then set the boy down on the floor. He immediately crawled toward the sofa.

The most comfortable looking piece of furniture was a rocking chair that didn't match the fancier pieces. Before it was a low footstool, just high enough to keep a woman's feet above the drafts that run along floors. She wondered whether Bess had made the embroidered footstool cover and the matching sewing bag that hung beside the chair.

Chase must have seen her looking at the rocking chair. "Tom surprised her with that chair right before their oldest, Aaron, was born. Nearest railroad station was at Benson back then, thirty miles from here, so that's the closest he could have the chair shipped. Tom and me took a buckboard to pick up a load of wood and came back with the wood and the chair both. There was no road between our settlement and Benson back then. Just ruts across the prairie." A grin split his wide face. "That chair rocked so hard it had twice as many miles as the buckboard by the time we reached here. Tom nearly burst with anticipation. All he could talk about was what Bess would say. Wish you could have seen Bess's face when we pulled up in front of the soddy with that chair."

Lorette tried to will away the knot that caught high in her chest. Chase's grin had gentled into a shadowy smile, and his eyes had the faraway look that eyes take on when one is watching memories. Lorette wished desperately that those memories were hers. She forced herself to smile. "I expect Tom wasn't disappointed in Bess's reaction?"

Chase chuckled, and she found her smile widening at the sound. "No. He surely was not. I can see her now, standing in front of that soddy with her apron and hair blowing in the wind. She took one look at the chair and her eyes grew as large as buggy wheels. Then she came across the yard as fast as her delicate condition allowed. Tom's boots had barely touched ground when her arms went around his neck. She like to squeezed the living daylights out of him."

Lorette studied his face, curious at the way his voice had softened at the end.

A large picture in an oval tortoise-shell frame caught her eye. She walked toward it slowly. It hung above a sideboard, another reminder that the little house did not have a proper dining room.

She hugged herself tightly as she stared at the family photograph. Bess's face, her beautiful, thick brown hair pulled severely back into a bun, stared back at her. Tom stood behind Bess with one hand on her shoulder, a proud young family man. Samuel's older brother and sister stood one on each side of Bess, leaning against their mother's lap. Bess held Samuel, his long embroidered gown cascading like a beautiful waterfall over Bess's dark tailored skirt. The children all had blond hair like their father. Lorette shivered and hugged herself even tighter.

"That was taken a couple months ago." Chase spoke from behind her in a low voice.

"I know." Her voice came out in a hoarse whisper. "She sent me a small copy of it."

Between Chase and Lorette hung a heavy, awkward silence, so common when one has lost a loved one and there is nothing anyone can say or do to bring them back or prevent the grief of their loss. Lorette stared at the picture, trying to absorb everything she could about her older sister. Bess had looked so different when she left Boston years ago as a young bride.

"She was happy." Chase's voice was gentle in its masculinity. "She loved being a mother and she loved Tom. She even loved this impossible-to-tame prairie."

"Her letters were filled with her joy."

Crash!

Lorette whirled about. Samuel was proudly surveying the sewing basket he'd tipped over. He reached eagerly for a ball of pale blue yarn stuck through with knitting needles that had tumbled from the

34

basket. Lorette darted forward, but Chase reached the boy first.

"That's not a toy, fella." Chase righted the basket and began replacing the spilled objects. "I'll keep him entertained if you want to look around a bit more."

A dainty ladies' desk stood beside a window. Curiosity stirred within Lorette. What reminders of herself had her sister left in that desk? Lorette crossed to it.

"Bess wrote her letters to you seated there."

Lorette took a bundle of envelopes from a cubbyhole, recognized her own handwriting on the top envelope, and quickly returned them to their keeping place. She pulled out a drawer. She didn't know what she expected to see there, but what she found was a book bound in rich brown leather. Curious, she removed and opened it.

This will be our first night sleeping in our new home. It's been a long day and my eyes are closing in exhaustion as I write, but I could not go to bed without recording the great joy Tom and I are feeling this day.

Tears blurred the script. Lorette returned the journal to the drawer. She knew that later she would read and cherish this record of Bess's thoughts. Yet Lorette's pain was still too new to read it now. She closed the drawer and turned her back to the desk.

Chase was on the floor beside Samuel. Four wooden blocks sat in a row on the thick brown rug. Chase slowly balanced a block on top of the others. "See, Sam? It's easy." He placed another block.

Samuel stared, his brown eyes wide below lifted blond brows, his little bow mouth open slightly.

"Going to help me, Sam?" Chase placed one of Samuel's hands on a block. Together they lifted and placed it.

Chase's tanned hand seemed to swallow up Samuel's tiny white one. Lorette smiled at the sweetness of the moment. With a pleasant start she realized that for the first time in days she was genuinely smiling inside, too. The smile loosened somewhat the painful knot that had existed in her chest since hearing of Bess's death.

Lorette wasn't accustomed to seeing men play with their children. The fathers of the children for whom she had cared in Philadelphia had been reserved with their offspring. Had Tom played with Samuel,

Aaron, and Liza as Chase was playing now? If so, the children had indeed been blessed.

"We did it, Sam," Chase congratulated.

Samuel stared at the blocks a moment longer. Bending forward suddenly he pushed the block they had so carefully balanced in place with the palm of his hand. The block went tumbling. Samuel giggled and slapped his hands on his chubby knees, his face filled with glee.

"Hey!" Chase's face registered disbelief.

Lorette burst into laughter at his chagrin. Chase looked up in surprise. Meeting her gaze, he joined in her laughter.

He stood to his feet, bending over to swoop Samuel into one arm. "Guess the fellow isn't into building yet." He disentangled a hunk of his hair from one of Samuel's fists. "How are things going at the Henrys'?"

"They are no longer 'going' at all." She held out her arms for Samuel.

Blond brows met above troubled eyes. "Haven't they treated you well? Mr. Henry has a fine reputation —"

"Oh, yes," she hurried to assure him. "They simply wish for a governess who can give all her attention to their children." She touched her lips lightly to Samuel's temple. "I can't do that." She glanced into the boy's bright eyes and smiled. "Thank God, I cannot do that," she whispered.

Chase stuffed his hands into his trouser pockets. "Will you be taking Sam back to Philadelphia?"

He stood in an easy manner, but she sensed a tension about him. Was he afraid she would take the only remaining member of his friends' family away?

"Maybe," Lorette responded. "But parents back East don't care for governesses who come with nephews any more than parents here. I'll need to find another way to support us."

"So . . . what are you planning?"

"The attorney read the will to me yesterday. He said Samuel inherits this house and farm."

"And?"

Lorette shrugged. "My first thought was to sell the farm. The money from the sale would be Samuel's, of course. It would all go for his support."

He nodded, his gaze on hers.

"If I can't find another position where I can keep him with me, I can use the money to pay someone else to care for him properly while I work. Or perhaps the money would allow me to stay with him until he is old enough to begin school before I accept another position as a governess."

She waited, hoping for a response from him. He'd been Tom's best friend. Wouldn't he know what Tom and Bess would have wanted her to do?

"I'm afraid the farm wouldn't bring as much money as you think." Chase sounded as though he spoke with reluctance.

Unease quickened her heartbeat. "Why not?"

"Tom made a good start developing this place, but it took a heap of money to do it. Sam must have inherited Tom's debts. Selling the farm would barely pay them off."

"How can that be? They homesteaded the land. It barely cost them anything." Lorette spread her free hand to indicate the home within which they stood. "They had enough money to buy and furnish this new house."

"He used the land and future crops to borrow the money to pay for the house, and for farm machinery to run this place, and to buy another section of land."

His words sent goose bumps running along her arms, and she shivered. "What about the crops? Won't they help pay the debts?"

"It's not as simple as it sounds. Farmers live on credit all year. It's not only the house and machinery they pay for after harvest. If the crops are poor, prices will be good — that is, if you're one of the fortunate farmers with crops to sell. If the crops are good, prices will be low because everyone has a lot to sell. Either way, there won't be enough to pay off normal living debts and the loans, too. 'Course if you're thrifty, there may be enough to pay off this year's loan payments."

The hope in Lorette's chest was rapidly sinking. "I suppose I could rent the farm out. It wouldn't support Samuel and me, but it would help pay the debts and let us keep the farm for Samuel."

"Sure. 'Course, if the renter doesn't pay up or the crops aren't good in the future, you'll need to find another way to make the loan payments or lose the property."

Lorette closed her hands into fists in frustration. "How do farmers manage to live at all?"

He grinned. "Tom always said the only way was by depending on God and using a man's brains and brawn. I'd say he's right."

"But what am I going to do?"

"If you don't mind a suggestion —"

"Mind? I'm pleading for one."

"You don't need to decide this minute. You can stay here while you figure things out. You and Sam would have a roof over your heads and a garden and chickens and a cow for your meals."

"I don't know anything about running a farm. I wouldn't have one idea of what to do with the crops."

"I do."

She stared at him a moment, not comprehending his quiet reply. Understanding dawned rapidly. "Oh. *Oh.* The chickens . . . the cow . . . the other animals . . . *you* have been caring for them the last couple weeks."

Chase shifted his feet and glanced at the floor. "Yes."

"And the crops?"

Chase nodded.

"Oh, my." Lorette moved to the dainty rocking chair and sank onto the tapestry covering. "My thoughts have been only on my grief and Samuel's, and on how I am going to care for Samuel. I've been incredibly selfish, leaving the care of this place on your shoulders. I'll pay you for your trouble. I have a little money coming from the two weeks I spent with the Henrys."

41

He shook his head vigorously. "I couldn't take the money. I've done what I've done for Tom. He was a good friend. If you decide to move in here for a while I'll be more than glad to continue helping you out."

Everything in Lorette's nature went against accepting such a huge gift, but she knew she must accept it out of concern for Samuel's future. If what Chase said about the crops and debt were true, she'd need her meager funds.

"Thank you. I accept your kind offer." She forced a smile. "I'm afraid you've no idea how much your advice will be needed. I know nothing of life on a farm. In Philadelphia my food came from merchants, not from the land just outside my door."

"You'll catch on."

He sounded as though he had no doubt at all. She wished she were as sure of her capabilities.

At least for the moment, she and Samuel had a roof over their heads and food for only the price of her labor. She needn't worry immediately about finding a position, nor must she rely on Kari Bresven's or the Henrys' charity to meet her own and Samuel's needs. Some of her trepidation at staying on the farm melted away. Depending on Chase Lankford to help her with the farm, she felt as secure as Samuel obviously felt when in Chase's arms.

Chase rolled over, grunting when his shoulder hit a raised nail. He shifted. The wooden floor he'd put in his sod house was a pleasure to walk on, but there was no way to make it comfortable for sleeping. Still, he didn't regret giving the feather mattress from his bed to Lorette. He smiled into the night, playing her name over in his mind. Manners might demand that he refer to her as Miss Taber, but in the privacy of his thoughts he loved the sound of her name.

He hadn't told Lorette that the mattress was his. She'd assumed Mrs. Bresven had lent it, along with the Swedish woman's pillow, sheets, and quilts. He hadn't informed her otherwise. The bedding had been necessary to replace that which the doctor had ordered him to burn.

Chase rolled over again and groaned. He'd order another mattress next time he was in town. At least he still had a pillow.

He let the events of the afternoon roll through his mind. Since their deaths, it had been difficult to be in the home of Tom and Bess. He still missed them sorely.

43

He supposed he would feel that way for a long time.

Still, the sound of Lorette's laughter rang in his memory, and he pictured her face when he'd looked up from playing with Sam. It had been a perfect moment.

The picture was replaced by the sadness he'd caught in her blue eyes. Seeing that pain, his instinct had been to try to protect her, the same way he wanted to protect Sam. It was then that the thought of marriage first crossed his mind.

Foolish thought. Pity was no foundation for marriage. Besides, he couldn't protect her. Not by marriage or any other way. Not only hadn't he the right, the same as he hadn't the right to protect Sam, but grief wasn't a pain from which anyone could be protected by another human being.

When Lorette said she might take Sam back East to raise, he'd felt a pain in his stomach worse than the worst sickness he'd ever known. He'd had to all but bite his tongue to keep from asking her to marry him right then.

He snorted and drew his quilt up to his chin. Didn't make any sense to ask a woman he barely knew to marry him, even if Bess had been telling him about Lorette for years. He might not have known

Lorette long, but he'd seen enough to admire her pluck. He was glad she wasn't the kind of woman who'd consider Sam's inheritance something to feather her own nest. And she sure wasn't sore on the eyes.

The only other woman he'd ever thought of marrying was Anna, and he'd known her for years before he asked. She had turned him down flat. A life of a farmer's wife was too hard, she'd said.

So he'd taken up his homestead claim and closed his heart.

Until now. Until Lorette.

He snorted again. No reason in the world to believe she'd have said yes to his proposal even if he'd been rash enough to make it.

He dug his head deeper into the pillow and muttered, "Must be lonelier than I realized to even invent such a thought."

While the vision of Lorette's eyes played in his thoughts, Chase drifted into sleep.

Chapter 3

The dawn streamed through the lace-covered windows as Lorette arose early the next morning. The sweet music of Samuel's baby jabberings drifted from his cradle beside her bed, providing a pleasant start to her day. She talked with him while she dressed, glad he never seemed hungry until he'd been up for a while.

"You're such a good-natured little boy." She ran a hand over the cradle's hooded bonnet with its carving of roses. The wood was butter smooth. Tom must have sanded it for hours and hours. "Your mother wrote me about this cradle, how your father made it and gave it to your mother the Christmas they were expecting Aaron."

Samuel grinned and kicked his feet.

Lorette wondered whether Samuel could feel his father's love surrounding him when he was in the cradle. Her eyes misted over, and she brushed at them with the back of her hand.

Putting behind her fanciful thoughts, she picked up Samuel and started downstairs. The two rooms behind closed doors across the hall were hard to ignore. She had peaked into them last night. They felt forlorn with mattressless bedsteads and deserted toys: one of Liza's dolls, a slingshot of Aaron's, and a pile of pebbles and arrowheads Aaron had collected. More than anything else, those rooms told the extent to which death had filled this house.

Lorette found Bess's aprons hanging on pegs on the pantry door. She reached for a crisp white apron, then selected a tan plaid which wouldn't show the inevitable results of a day's work as easily. Besides, it complemented her brown-checkered gingham dress, the simplest she owned.

While Samuel played with spoons on the floor, Lorette searched the pantry, discovering what she did and did not have available to prepare meals. She looked in wooden boxes, colorful tins, glass containers, cupboards, and drawers.

Finally she settled her hands on her hips.

"Well, Samuel, the only loaf of bread is moldy. Chase must not have thought to clean out the pantry when he disinfected the house. I find flour, but no yeast. We'll have to do without bread this morning. Rather, I will. Milk will satisfy you for a while."

She grunted as she lifted Samuel. "My, you're a big boy."

He grinned as though he appreciated her comment, then leaned forward and gave a harmless bite to her shoulder.

"You must be hungry. Or your new little teeth are bothering you." She picked up a small tin pail and he transferred his attention to it. "It's a good thing Chase showed me last night where the milk was kept or you'd miss breakfast, too," she continued, carrying him out to the well. "I'd never have guessed to look in the well. In Philadelphia, a delivery man brought milk to the house each day."

She set Samuel down in order to free both hands to raise the covered tin bucket of milk from the well. She poured enough milk for Samuel and to make pancakes for herself, then lowered the bucket back into the well. "I hope Chase . . . Mr. Lankford stops by this morning. This milk won't last you the day, Samuel."

She swung the boy up to her hip and groaned. His navy blue dress was covered with dirt. She'd been so intent on getting the milk she'd forgotten to pay attention. "At least it's not mud," she muttered, brushing him off.

Her stomach was growling by the time he'd had his fill of breakfast milk and she'd laid him in the crib in the corner of the kitchen for a nap. In the pen were a tin rattle and a rag doll which had seen better days, likely because it was well-loved.

Ready to make her own breakfast, she sighed. She couldn't make buckwheat cakes without eggs, and the eggs were in the sod barn beneath chickens. Lorette straightened her shoulders. "Trying to avoid the task, aren't you? What is so scary? Hundreds of women collect eggs every day. Thousands, maybe. Children, too." She picked up a basket from the counter and groaned. "Why doesn't that make me feel any braver?"

Lorette started across the yard, swinging the basket, deliberately putting a bounce in her step, and began singing "Oh, Susannah." Her spirits actually lifted until she opened the door to the sod barn.

"Oh! No! No! Oh!" Chickens and a rooster rushed at her, their cackles and feathered bodies filling the air. She threw her arms up, dropping the basket.

Strong arms drew her back. "Don't be afraid, Lorette. They only want to get outside and have their breakfast."

She clasped her palms over her racing heart. "Chase . . . Mr. Lankford, I'm so glad you're here. I . . . I don't know anything about chickens and . . . and eggs and . . . Can you show me what to do?"

She hated her breathlessness, but considering that a feathered army had just attacked her, she felt she was doing quite well.

Then she realized one of his large, strong hands was against her back, steadying her. A flush seemed to rise from the soles of her feet and spread upward to her hairline. She felt herself stiffen as though she were a statue.

He didn't appear to notice. With one easy movement, he leaned down, picked up her forgotten basket, and handed it to her.

"You'll be an old hand at egg hunting in no time."

Strong barnyard smells that she knew must be from the chickens, cow, two oxen, horse, straw, and things she didn't want to think about hung about them as they entered the building.

Even with his help, she definitely did *not* feel like an old hand at egg-gathering after they had collected eight brown eggs. "I feel like I've spent a week trying to keep a room full of eleven-year-old boys still and teach them arithmetic." It was the most tiring experience she could recall.

His laugh rang out clearly in the morning air.

Cheered, she tucked back a strand of hair loosened by the battle with the chickens and started toward the house.

"Uh . . . the chickens need feeding, Miss Taber."

She stopped short. "Oh. Of course."

"I'll show you where the feed is kept. You'll be giving them table scraps, too, naturally." He led her to a large wooden covered box, which stood along one wall.

"Naturally." Her ignorance was beginning to overwhelm her.

"Not everything, of course, but things like potato skins."

"Of course." Behind his back she rolled her eyes. She assumed he meant no meat scraps.

"Moo-oo-oo."

He turned to the cow. "Pansy." His face had the strangest expression.

"Is something wrong?"

He avoided her gaze and kept his own on the cow in the nearby stall. "Have you given Sam any milk yet today?"

"Yes. I'm glad you reminded me. I've used almost all the milk from the bucket in the well."

"There's more where that came from." His voice tangled with laughter, and his mouth twisted in a vain effort to avoid grinning.

Embarrassment flooded her. She felt so inadequate for the demands of farm living. "I know." She straightened her shoulders, attempting to retain a little dignity. "The trouble is, I don't know how to . . . to get at it."

Chase shouted with laughter. Within moments he was doubled-over in his mirth.

Lorette's embarrassment multiplied one hundred fold, but Chase's laughter was contagious, and soon she was laughing along with him. By the time their laughter had dissolved into chuckles, her sides hurt and she was wiping tears from her lashes.

"Let's feed the chickens," Chase said when they were both able to speak again. "Then I'll show you how to milk Pansy. She needs to be milked twice a day, every day. Each morning after milking let her out to pasture. You'll bring her in every evening and milk her again."

She recalled his milking lesson two weeks later while leaning against Pansy's side, feeling the occasional swat of Pansy's sharp, scratchy tail against her cheek and listening to the satisfying sound of milk entering the pail. Deep satisfaction filled her upon mastering this task, which people had been performing for thousands of years. She'd been surprised at the strength it took. Her wrists had been swollen at the end of that first day.

The milking done, she stood stiffly, put her hands on her lower back, and stretched. The gardening, house-work, and care of the animals were all taking their toll on her body. Her work as a governess seemed idle by comparison.

She pulled the heavy pail to safety. "We did well this morning, Pansy." The cow turned her huge head and eyed Lorette.

"Glad to hear it."

Lorette jumped, sloshing milk from the bucket onto her shoes. "Chase Lankford, you shouldn't startle a body so!"

"Sorry about the milk." Chase's grin showed he wasn't too sorry. He jostled Samuel, who was struggling unsuccessfully to get out of the man's arms and into the straw with the cats now winding about Chase's legs. "Stopped by the house. He was a bit perturbed at being there alone. Sounds like you're handling the milking just fine."

"Pansy didn't kick the bucket or step in it this morning. The cats didn't tip it trying to drink. Pansy didn't step on my foot or bump me off the stool. It's been my best milking yet." It was absurd how pleased it made her to tell him so.

"I knew you'd make a great milk maid." He ignored Samuel's continued efforts to get down.

Does he think I'm not caring for Samuel properly? she wondered uneasily. "I hate to leave Samuel in the crib while I do the chores, but it's too dangerous for him in the barn. One of the animals might kick him, or the chickens peck him." She shuddered at the things the straw hid. "I hate to think what he might try to put in his mouth." She poured the milk into the nearby strainer, then set down the empty pail and reached for the boy. "He does love to be close to the animals."

"Maybe I can make a small pen where he can play while you work in here, something smaller than his crib, maybe without legs. For now, if you want to give him breakfast, I'll finish up here for you."

Guilt and thankfulness braided together in an unlikely mix as she crossed the yard in a slow, stumbling gait with Samuel in one arm and a tin pail of milk in the opposite hand. She hated to allow Chase to do any of the chores she could do. He had so much to take care of with Tom's crops, as well as his own. Still, she was glad to be relieved from wiping that fierce-smelling concoction onto the animals. Chase said it helped keep the cow flies from biting them. She did pity Pansy, the oxen, and the horse, Boots, their constant battle with those creatures.

Lorette and Samuel had their share of the bites. She tried keeping herself and Samuel well-covered to prevent the bites, despite the summer heat. She resisted rubbing kerosene on herself and Samuel to keep the flies at bay as Chase and other farmers did. That was more than her Philadelphia-bred genteel self could bear.

At the porch outside the door, she slipped off her shoes. She had learned her first day on the farm what awful, smelly things her shoes accumulated in the barn. Today one of her shoes sloshed with spilled milk, too.

The fragrance of rising bread greeted her as she entered the house. Another lesson from Chase. When she'd told him she needed yeast to bake bread, he'd shown her Bess's supply of sourdough starter and how to make bread with it.

"Seems that man has had to teach me everything but how to change your diapers," she told Samuel, setting him on the kitchen floor.

She hadn't even known Bess had stored canned meats, vegetables, and fruit in the cellar until Chase told her so. She especially appreciated the canned meat. She hadn't been able to bring herself to kill a chicken yet. That was another thing Chase did. So far he had refrained from insisting she learn to do that herself.

She started a fire in the stove, then let it burn down to cooking and baking temperature while she fed Samuel. He was still fussy while he fed. He hadn't liked being weaned suddenly after his mother died. As she usually did, Lorette kept up a steady conversation with him while he drank the warm, fresh milk.

Samuel fell asleep with his blanket on the kitchen floor while she was putting the bread in the oven to bake. It was an overcast morning, and the baking wouldn't heat the house as unbearably as it did some days. Ready to begin breakfast for herself and Chase, she looked around for her eggs.

"I know I collected them. Where are they?" she muttered, glancing about the large kitchen. Then she remembered. Her hands full with Samuel and the milk, she hadn't had enough hands to carry the eggs from the barn to the house. She hated to leave Samuel, even when he was sleeping. But it would only take a moment to run to the barn.

She saw Chase turn about at the sound of her entering the sod barn. "I forgot the eggs." She headed quickly to where the basket sat on the straw-covered floor. She reached for the handle and saw something move quickly beneath the straw.

With a screech she leaped back. "A snake! It's a snake!"

Fear tore up through her like a living thing. She couldn't seem to move fast enough. Her feet felt as though they were in buckets. She couldn't take her gaze from the yellow form gliding through, blending in the straw. Her screams filled the barn and her ears and she couldn't stop them.

They continued while Chase grabbed a pitchfork, stabbed the wriggling form, and rushed outside with it. To Lorette it appeared he was moving at a snail's pace.

Lorette's screams turned into shaky gasps. She stumbled to the door, watching the floor the entire way, certain other snakes must be hiding in the innocent-looking straw covering. From outside she could hear Curly the dog barking excitedly.

She'd barely crossed the threshold when Chase's arms surrounded her, drawing her quivering body close. "It's all right," he whispered into her hair. "I killed the creature. It can't hurt you now."

Her fingers clutched at his shirt. "I've n–never seen a s–snake before. I didn't know there were s–snakes in the b–barn."

"It's just a corn snake."

Lorette thought it absurd to refer to any snake as "just" a snake.

One of Chase's large hands rubbed her back firmly but gently, and her shaking began to lessen. "Corn snakes are common in the fields, but they seldom come into the barn. The cats keep them away."

Even so, Lorette wondered how she would dare set foot in the barn again . . . or take the animals to pasture . . . or bring Chase his lunch in the fields. She didn't know how to tell him the extent of her fear. Bess and other women had lived with the reality of snakes in their world. Somehow she would have to find the strength to do so, too.

Chase's arms were so comforting. She had only experienced a man's arms about her a couple of times before. Never had they felt this strong, this gentle. Held close, her cheek against his shoulder, she could hide her embarrassment at the way she'd reacted, but she could not stay there. Reluctantly, she pushed herself away.

He released his hold immediately.

She wished he hadn't. *Don't be a silly goose,* she reprimanded herself. "Thank you for killing the snake. I'm afraid I'm rather timid when it comes to them. I never saw a snake in Philadelphia."

"Everyone jumps when they see a snake. It's human nature. Corn snakes aren't poisonous. There aren't any poisonous snakes hereabouts."

She appreciated his attempts to reassure her, but they weren't working. She glanced back at the sod barn door. Apprehension sent shivers through her. "Would you mind? The egg basket is still in there."

He retrieved it for her.

Her knees felt as pliant as corn silk as she walked to the house. Her hands shook when she slipped her shoes off on the porch.

Once inside, her hair stood on end. "Samuel! No!"

Chapter 4

Samuel was crawling across the kitchen floor, headed for the hot stove. Lorette dropped the basket and rushed for him, grabbing him up in a bear hug just as he reached out for the silver filigree on the oven door.

Samuel let out a squeal.

She only hugged him tighter. She took two steps back from the dangerous stove and dropped to her knees. Samuel squirmed. She didn't let go. "That's hot. Samuel must never touch the stove. Hot!" The words trembled, but no more than her heart. If she had been a moment later returning from the barn —

She couldn't let herself think of the "what-ifs." Thank God she'd returned in time. Her heart went out to all the mothers who hadn't.

Tears rolled over her cheeks. She rocked herself and Samuel back and forth, trying to comfort herself. *I can't do this,* she thought. *I can't live like this. It's too much. It's too hard, too dangerous.*

Eventually her sobs stopped, her breathing became normal, and her thoughts less wild. Hot stoves were in every house, not just prairie farmhouses, she reminded herself. There was no place she could take Samuel where there would not be dangers. Besides, she should not have left him alone on the floor, even though she had been certain he was sound asleep.

When her legs would hold her again, she put Samuel in his crib in the corner of the kitchen. He howled in protest until she brought him a pan lid and spoons to pound together.

Lorette rinsed her face with cold water, trying to wash away the vestiges of her crying jag, and straightened her hair, which had been mussed from rubbing against Chase's shirt. She felt her face burn at the memory.

Only then did she remember the egg basket. Most of the eggs were broken. A sticky yellow mess covered the bottom of the basket. She picked up the three eggs that remained whole, lifted her chin in determination, and began breakfast for herself and Chase.

She'd insisted Chase take his meals with them and that she would do his laundry in partial payment for all the work he did on the farm. She'd learned quickly that he liked a big breakfast after he'd done chores and before he left for the fields. Today she made fried potatoes, bacon, and the three eggs. Fresh warm bread and her own butter would round out the meal.

Truth be told, she enjoyed the time that she and Chase shared at meals. His companionship kept some of the loneliness of farm living from overwhelming her. She was accustomed to spending most of her days with children, but not to the exclusion of adult companionship.

Determined to put the morning's frightful memories behind her, she forced herself to sing. "What a friend we have in Jesus," she started, her voice quavering, "all our sins and griefs to bear." Before long, the quavering ceased. Samuel kept up a beat on a pan lid that was like no accompaniment Lorette had sung to in the past. By the time Chase came to the house for breakfast, Lorette had herself well in hand.

"It's nice to hear singing in this house again," Chase said when they sat down to eat. "Your sister sang while she worked, too."

Lorette's smile was genuine. His memories of Bess were different than Lorette's, but she was glad they shared memories of her. "Tell me more about her, the way you knew her."

He did. The things he remembered might have seemed insignificant to others, but to Lorette they spoke loudly of Bess's love for Tom and the children and her joy in the life she lived.

Lorette wondered silently whether a corn snake had ever surprised Bess, and if so, how she'd reacted. Lorette doubted her older sister had fallen apart and ended up in the arms of a man to whom she wasn't married for comfort.

The thought brought back the wonderful sense of rightness and security she'd felt in Chase's arms, the strength in the arms hidden beneath the brown cotton shirtsleeves. She had to lower her gaze to her plate to keep her eyes from revealing her thoughts to the man across the small table.

He didn't appear to notice anything unusual in the atmosphere between them. His mind was apparently on more practical things.

"Looks like it might rain later today. Might take advantage of the weather to drive into town and take care of some business. You're welcome to join me, if you'd like."

Lorette looked up in surprise. "In the rain?"

He shrugged. "If it's raining more than a drizzle, I can't be in the fields. If you'd rather not ride in the rain, you can give me a list of things you need and I'll pick them up."

"Oh, no, I don't mind the rain." She wasn't about to pass up a trip to town, regardless of the weather.

After the breakfast dishes were cleared, she examined the items in the pantry and made a list, just in case the trip became reality. Her mood lifted by the minute. She'd taken to wearing Bess's housedresses, as they were more suitable than most of the clothes she'd brought from Philadelphia. Now she changed from Bess's worn housedress to one of her own simple gowns, one that wouldn't be ruined by a little rain. Even Samuel had a change of dress.

Her spirits continued to lighten as the sky grew darker and sprinkles pattered against the windows. She stood in the kitchen doorway and watched the clouds tumble over each other across the sky, glorying in the vast distance she could see above the rolling prairie lands. The smell of rain and wet earth and grasses was refreshing.

In an effort to still her impatience and to keep Samuel entertained and clean until they left, she settled herself and Samuel in Bess's rocking chair with Bess's journal. Lorette had begun the practice of reading aloud to Samuel from the journal the first full day she'd spent in the house.

A small crocheted white cross marked the place she'd left off at the last reading. She started the chair in its gentle rocking motion while she opened the book.

Mr. Lankford had dinner with us today following church services. Afterward, while I cleaned up the kitchen, he and Tom rolled about the floor with Aaron and Liza for all the world as though they were children themselves. Aaron and Liz love Mr. Lankford as though he were one of us. He is a hard-working, responsible man, a

65

church-going man, gentle yet strong in his ways.

Lorette was glad for the journal's glimpses into Bess's view of Chase. Her mind drifted to the man who had become such a large part of her life in such a short time. She might as well admit that she not only relied upon him, but she was beginning to care deeply for him — and as more than just a friend.

"Don't fool yourself into thinking he helps out for you," she admonished herself. "He does it for Samuel and because Tom was his friend."

She started as the kitchen door slammed. "Miss Taber? Are you ready to leave for town?" Chase called as he entered the house.

When she and Samuel joined Chase, she was surprised to see a buggy drawn up to the porch. "I didn't know Tom and Bess had a buggy."

"I borrowed it from the Bresvens. Figured you and Sam would get soaked riding in the wagon."

Even with the covered buggy, their ride was a damp one. She was glad for the oil-cloth Chase provided to cover their legs and laps.

Bess's journal entry and the minutes Lorette spent in Chase's arms that morning made Lorette all the more conscious of every bounce of the wagon that jostled her shoulder into his. Her heart kept an erratic pace during the journey. She couldn't help but wonder whether the simple, innocent contact reminded him of the time they'd spent in each other's arms, too.

The muddy roads made the journey longer than usual, and Lorette thought they made the ride bumpier than usual, also. Conversation with Chase was somewhat limited. It took all of Chase's concentration to drive as the road grew worse.

The simple general store with its narrow aisles and one room of goods piled upon goods from floor to ceiling looked as wonderful to Lorette as a large emporium in downtown Philadelphia. Chase introduced her to the owner, a middle-aged Swedish man named Larson. Chase explained that she was Tom's sister-in-law, and Larson agreed to extend her credit against harvest.

Lorette and Chase went about the store gathering items from their separate lists. Chase completed his within minutes. "I'm having a leather harness repaired at a shop down the street. I'll run down and pick it up while you finish here."

She agreed and went happily back to examining the bolts of fabric piled on a table in one corner of the store. Samuel was growing fast. He would need new clothes soon.

"How nice to see you, Miss Taber."

Lorette turned to the woman at her elbow. "Mrs. Henry, what a pleasant surprise."

Mrs. Henry leaned forward and tickled Samuel's cheek with a gloved index finger. "Hello there, Samuel. My, aren't you the big boy." She straightened and smiled her formal smile at Lorette. "I hope things are going well for you on the farm, my dear."

"Yes, everything is fine." *Mrs. Henry's words are always right,* Lorette thought, *but somehow her manner makes them sound all wrong.* "How are the children?"

"Fine, fine." Mrs. Henry waved her hand in a dismissing manner. A frown marred her features. "There's something I must tell you." Her voice had dropped a degree.

At her tone, Lorette's stomach turned queasy. She tried to ignore it. What could the woman possibly say that could justify such a feeling? Lorette barely knew the woman. "What is that, Mrs. Henry?"

Mrs. Henry laid a hand on Lorette's

forearm. "My dear, I hardly know how to say this."

Lorette wished her former employer would stop calling her "my dear." "Say what?"

"I understand Mr. Lankford spends a great deal of time at your farm."

"Yes. He's been a marvelous help. As you know, I know nothing of running a farm."

"He was a friend of your brother-in-law's, of course."

"Yes. They helped each other with their fields, so Mr. Lankford knows all about Tom's crops."

Mrs. Henry bit her bottom lip for a moment. "People say Mr. Lankford spends a *great* deal of time at your farm." She hesitated, staring directly into Lorette's eyes. "An inordinate amount of time."

The woman's meaning began to sink in. Lorette could hear a roaring sound in her ears. "What are you saying?" Her lips felt numb, but she knew she had asked the question. If Mrs. Henry was saying what Lorette thought, she needed to hear it in plain English.

"People are saying he is living at the farm with you, that you are living together . . . inappropriately."

Chapter 5

The ride back to the farm was the longest Chase could ever remember. The man at the saddle shop had told him of the ugly rumor going about town. Chase knew there were men who found such tales amusing, but he could hardly believe the townspeople he knew and respected thought him capable of such gross conduct.

Worse, they thought sweet Lorette would descend to such an arrangement.

The entire situation made him sick.

He'd told the leather worker, in no uncertain terms, that the rumors were not true. Chase had no illusions that he would be able to squelch the rumors or convince everyone of their untruth. He knew enough about human nature to know he could not work such miracles.

Anger at what the rumors would mean to Lorette's reputation made him drive Boots harder than he normally would under such poor road conditions. His thoughts swirled in a vicious circle. What was he going to do? What could he do? Did Lorette know? Had she, too, heard the rumors in town? She seemed agitated, avoiding his glance, barely speaking, but perhaps she was only responding to his temperament, which he admitted to himself was anything but friendly and easy-going.

Lorette was glad when they finally arrived back at the farm and Chase headed to the Bresvens' with the buggy. The ride had seemed unendurable. The rumor had shouted through her mind the entire time.

Had Chase heard the awful accusations? "Oh, no." She stopped short. Did he think she had staged her fright at the snake that morning, had purposely found a reason to throw herself into his arms? The possibility was too horrible to consider.

"How can people be so terrible, making up stories like this about people?" she asked the Lord, unpacking the goods from the wooden box Chase had carried into the house for her.

It was awful enough for her and for Chase, but it almost broke her heart to think what the rumors would mean for Samuel. The sins of the fathers did follow the children. The untrue rumors would follow Samuel if he grew up here. What would Bess think if she knew the disgrace Lorette and Chase had inadvertently brought upon her youngest son? The thought twisted Lorette's heart like a cloth being wrung.

"I thought You would make a way for Samuel and me, Lord. Is this hurtful rumor Your way of telling me that Samuel and I are to move back to Philadelphia? Please, make our path clear, so I do not make any more missteps."

The next morning Chase arrived as Lorette was headed to the barn to care for the animals. Did she only imagine that his face looked grim and gray circles underscored his normally smiling eyes?

"I'll take care of the animals this morning." His tone sounded curt.

She longed to take him up on his offer but knew she didn't dare. "If I don't find the courage to go back in the barn today, I might never find it."

For a moment she didn't think he was going to accept her decision. Then he nodded. "We'll work together. You collect the eggs and milk Pansy while I rub the animals down with the fly ointment."

Gratitude flooded her. In spite of her brave words, she was terrified to step into the straw that hid snakes and other creatures so well. "Thank you."

He glanced at Samuel, who was seated on her hip, and raised his eyebrows.

Lorette explained about the stove incident from the day before. "I don't dare leave him alone in the house anymore. He's not satisfied with crawling any longer. He pulls himself up on everything. Any day now he'll be walking."

When they were done with the chores Chase carried the milk to the house while Lorette carried Samuel and the eggs. "I won't be needing any breakfast this morning," he said without meeting her gaze. "Fields are too wet to get into today. I'll be using the time to mend some things about my own place."

He turned abruptly, leaving before she could say good-bye.

The day wore on drearily long. Lunch and dinner seemed too much work to prepare for only herself. She settled for bread with butter and sugar and didn't bother to cook. She was glad when it was time to bring the animals back from pasture, even though it also meant entering the barn again, and this time without Chase's comforting presence.

She was inordinately pleased to find Chase's wagon in the yard and Chase in the barn when she returned. He was raking an area clear of straw. With a wave of his hand he indicated a legless wooden pen similar to the crib in the kitchen. "Thought we'd better set up a safe place for Sam in here right away."

"Thank you. I know how difficult it must have been for you to find time for this."

"Needed doing."

She set Samuel in the pen and went to get a pail of water from the well. The animals' legs and undersides were mud-caked from being in the pasture after yesterday's rain. Pansy's udders needed washing before milking.

Once she started milking, Lorette was so busy watching the floor for snakes that the milk bucket was missed as often as it was hit. She gritted her teeth and forced her attention on her work.

She and Chase worked in silence, at least

in as much silence as one could find in a barn with a cow, oxen, a horse, chickens, insects, a woman milking, a man raking and tossing straw, and a ten-month-old boy trying to get anyone's and anything's attention. Lorette wondered how one small earthen building could hold so much tension. Then she wondered how her much smaller body could contain that much tension.

Still in silence, Chase accompanied her and Samuel to the house. He set the milk down on the porch. "We need to talk."

His demanding tone surprised her. "All right. Let me get a shawl to protect Samuel from the gnats."

He was pacing the porch when she returned. He stopped a foot from her. In the twilight the lines in his face looked set in stone. "I don't know if you heard the rumors in town yesterday —"

She nodded, too embarrassed to answer.

His shoulders lowered slightly, and she knew he was relieved not to have to put the rumor into words for her. "I haven't been able to think of anything else since I heard them."

"It's been the same for me," she admitted.

"I think I have a solution."

Immediately her spirits brightened. "Yes?" She should have known he would come up with something. Hadn't he had an answer for all her problems from the very beginning?

He took a deep breath. His hands formed into fists at his sides. "Marriage. I mean, I think we should marry. That is, will you marry me? Please, Miss Taber?"

Shock rolled through her. Her mouth dropped open. She couldn't make her throat work. Her first thought was to blurt out that of course she could not marry him, but something within her checked the words. It couldn't have been easy for him to offer this proposal. Her answer should be as kind as she could make it.

Lorette had to swallow twice before she could speak. She lifted her chin and straightened her shoulders in an attempt to gather as much dignity as possible about her. "It's kind of you to try to save my reputation from the rumors, Mr. Lankford. However, I assure you — your generous sacrifice is not necessary."

"I'm not asking because of your reputation. Well, not entirely, though I've seen how easy it is for a woman's reputation to be ruined. I'm thinking mostly of young

Sam. His life might be affected by these rumors, too."

Lorette turned and stared out over the farmyard to keep him from seeing that she recognized the truth of his words. "I can take him back East."

She felt his hand firm and gentle on her shoulder and caught her breath sharply.

"Miss Taber." His voice was as gentle as his touch. "Together we can make good parents for Sam, and if we're married, I can stick around to help you run Sam's farm."

Unexpected pain ripped through her. His arguments were true, but they weren't what her heart wanted to hear. She had always dreamed of her future husband expressing undying love for her when he proposed marriage. This man only wanted a ready-made family, and a housekeeper, and maybe Samuel's farm.

No, that's not true, her heart forced her to admit, *not the part about Samuel's farm.*

Lorette wished Chase would remove his hand from her shoulder. His touch made it more difficult to think clearly. But what was there to think about? There could only be one answer.

She pulled her shawl more tightly about

her and Samuel. The boy nestled against her chest, his eyelashes resting against his fat cheeks as he drifted off to sleep. If only she were as restful.

"I know you love Samuel, Mr. Lankford, and it's a fine thing you are willing to raise him as your own." She did love the way he loved the boy. "Even so, my answer to your proposal is . . . no." It was harder to say than she'd anticipated.

He took a deep breath. "I understand your reluctance, Miss Taber, but my proposal stands, should you change your mind."

His boots clumped against the porch's wooden planks as he left. She watched him, barely more than a dark shadow against the twilight skies, as he walked down the rutted dirt road toward his neighboring farm. Finally, as he crossed a cornfield a bend hid him from sight.

She lowered herself slowly onto the top step. Her thoughts reeled. The same questions and the same problems and the same possibilities replayed over and over while the twilight faded into night and the nighttime insects' songs grew loud. Samuel's breathing grew slower and more even, his tiny chest rising and falling rhythmically against her own. Curly laid down beside her, resting his head against her thigh with a melodramatic sigh.

Like most unmarried women her age, Lorette had dreamed for years of marrying. Even in a large city like Philadelphia, a governess had few opportunities to meet marriageable men. Properly chaperoning and teaching children did not include becoming overly friendly with vendors and clerks. The few men who had asked to escort her she had met at church. Most were widowers looking for someone to care for their homes and raise their children. She'd wanted more in a marriage. She'd wanted a man who wanted her for herself. "Is that so much to ask, Lord? Is it terribly selfish to want to be loved for me?" she whispered into the night.

Curly stirred, looking up at her with a soft whine. She smiled down at him. "It's all right," she assured him quietly. "I'm only indulging in a little self-pity."

The night was clear and the stars sparkled with more brilliance than a Philadelphia jeweler's window. She loved the prairie sky. She couldn't remember it ever looking so large back East. It reminded her of the entry she'd read in Bess's diary that day.

Each day as I look out over this vast land, I am amazed anew at what Tom and I and others like us are accomplishing, the homes and communities we are building on this prairie. The sky, the fields, the prairie grasses seem to go on forever. When our children are grown, will there be any wild land left to tame? I hope the children will still be able to feel the wonder of this place. Today when Tom came in from the fields, Aaron ran to greet him and asked when he can be a farmer. I thought Tom would burst from pride that his son at even such a young age wants to work alongside him. Will our boys still want to work beside Tom in the fields when they are grown? At least in this fine land they will have the opportunity to do so if they choose.

Lorette had told Chase she could take Samuel back East to protect him from the rumors about her and Chase. If she did, would Samuel have the opportunity to choose the life of his father, as Bess and Tom wished for the boy? Could she deny him the opportunity to claim the heritage for which they'd fought so hard for him?

If her refusal to marry Chase was the

right thing, why didn't she feel at peace? Instead she felt restless inside.

Lorette pressed a soft kiss to Samuel's head. She loved the way he rested against her with complete abandon, with complete trust. She couldn't imagine a better man than Chase to raise him. She hadn't a doubt Tom and Bess would approve. Chase would make an honorable and faithful husband. "But, Lord, I don't know if I can give up the dream of marrying a man who loves me."

Even for Samuel? The words whispered through her mind.

She'd asked the Lord yesterday to make clear the best path for her and Samuel. Was marriage to Chase His answer?

Chapter 6

Chase risked a glance at Lorette over the breakfast table. She didn't meet his glance. Her gaze was on her plate, where she idly pushed a piece of sausage about with her fork.

Gray circles shaded the area beneath her eyes. She looked like she hadn't slept any better than he had last night. Could she have reconsidered his proposal? He didn't have the courage to ask, and she didn't mention it.

They barely spoke two words to each other all morning, not during the barn chores and not since. The silence between them was thicker than cream, and not nearly so pleasant.

He glanced down at his own plate and

realized he hadn't eaten any more than Lorette. He took a bite of fried egg. Cold fried egg.

Misery slithered through his chest. He'd enjoyed Lorette's company almost from the beginning. Had he ruined all chance of friendship between them by his proposal last night? He had convinced himself it was the sensible thing to do.

Lying in bed last night he finally admitted the truth to himself. He was falling in love with Lorette. He admired that she hadn't for a moment considered the possibility of not raising Sam, that she was willing to do anything necessary to care for him properly. He liked the courage with which she took to farm life. He enjoyed her cheerful companionship at meals each day.

And he couldn't bear the thought that not only Sam but Lorette might move east, out of his life forever. That fear had been behind his proposal. Had he been a fool to broach the subject of marriage?

Lorette cleared her throat.

His gaze darted to her.

She was still staring at her plate. "About last night . . ."

He waited.

She took a deep breath, not lifting her gaze. "I've been thinking. If I take Samuel back East, I'll likely have to sell the farm." Her words began to come in a rush. "I know from Bess's journal and letters that it was important to her and Tom that the children grow up out here. The farm is Samuel's heritage. I want him to have the choice of living here when he's grown. I know Tom and Bess would want that for him, too. I can't take that away from Samuel."

She paused again, pressing her lips together so hard they turned white. He could barely breathe for waiting for her to finish.

She took another deep breath. "So, if your offer still stands, for Samuel's sake, my answer is yes."

"Yes?"

Lorette nodded, lifting her lashes but not her head to peer at him, as if to judge his reaction.

"Yes." Joy relieved the pressure in his chest. "You said 'yes'?"

A smile tugged at the edges of her lips. Her gaze darted from one side to the other and back to him in an embarrassed manner that delighted him.

He reminded himself that she wasn't marrying him because she loved him, but for Sam's sake. It surprised him that the knowledge only slightly diminished his joy. "When?"

She shrugged, looking confused.

"It should be soon. To squelch the rumors, I mean."

A shadow passed over her face. He could have kicked himself. How could he be so insensitive? They both knew the rumors were the reason he'd proposed. No need to keep dragging them up. "Is this evening too soon?"

"This evening?" Her voice sounded small and frightened.

Was she frightened to marry him? The thought dampened his spirits. "We can go into town this morning for the license."

"What about the crops?"

"They'll have to do their growing without me this morning. Get yourself and Sam ready. I'll hitch Boots up to the wagon. I want to stop by Bresvens' on the way."

By the time they were ready to leave, Lorette had changed into a slim peach-colored dress with lace trim and a matching bonnet. The dress was much fancier than the calico and gingham dresses covered by aprons she normally wore about the farm. She blushed prettily when he complimented her.

Lorette waited in the wagon while he went to speak with Mrs. Bresven. When he told her of the marriage, the Swedish woman hesitated only a moment before her round face burst into a smile. Her plump hands clasped his arms. "The Bible says it's a good thing when a man finds a wife. You've found yourself a good one in Miss Taber. I'm happy for you both," she congratulated in her singsong accent.

The reserve with which he'd been protecting himself fell away. "Thank you. We want to get married right away. Tonight. I was wondering — could we be married in your parlor? I know it's a lot to ask on such short notice, but I want it to be special for her, and —"

"A wedding in my own parlor!" Her eyes sparkled. "Yah, I should say you can marry here."

She insisted on going out to the wagon to congratulate Lorette. They found the future Mrs. Lankford in the wagon bed finishing up changing Sam's diaper. Chase watched Lorette's face anxiously as Mrs. Bresven eagerly congratulated Lorette and told how honored she was that Chase and Lorette wanted to be married in the Bresvens' home.

Lorette's surprised gaze met Chase's

taken hours this afternoon to iron out the wrinkles.

"You look beautiful in it."

Lorette looked up in surprise at Chase's gravelly voice. She hadn't realized he was so close.

He cleared his throat. "Bess would have been happy that you chose to wear her wedding gown."

Lorette smiled at him, glad he recognized that wearing the dress made her feel closer to her sister.

The Bresven children rushed about alternately helping their mother prepare for company and reluctantly obeying her orders to keep away from the food and to be careful of their Sunday clothes. They all wanted to hold Samuel and play with him. Lorette enjoyed the bustle. The conversation with the children kept her mind off the enormity of the event ahead.

She was surprised when neighbors began stopping. "I thought only the Bresvens would be at the wedding," she said when she and Chase had a rare moment alone.

"I wanted my friends to celebrate with us. Do you mind very much?"

"No."

He touched her cheek softly with the

back of one hand. "I wish your friends could be here."

At the gentleness of his touch and his thought for her, sweet pain throbbed in her chest. Her gaze caught in his and she forgot there were other people about them.

"Here comes the minister," someone shouted.

The announcement jolted Lorette back to the parlor.

The ceremony was simple and solemn. Lorette was thankful that Chase had arranged for the minister to perform it, rather than the judge she had at first thought would marry them. She believed deeply that marriage was not only a legal but also a spiritual union.

It was frightening saying the vows, pledging to spend her life with this man she'd known such a short time. But working on the farm together, didn't they know each other better than most couples who courted in the prescribed manner?

She barely noticed the ring when he slipped it on her finger. When the ceremony was over and his friends were toasting them with Kari's punch, Lorette realized she was twisting the ring nervously and looked closer. She gasped at the beautiful jewelry. The stone was a large, rectangular blue sapphire mounted in a delicate, intricate setting. She looked up at Chase and saw he was watching her. He seemed to understand her question.

"The ring was my mother's," he said in low voice for her ears alone. "If you don't like it, we'll buy you another."

"No." She slid her right hand over the ring. "I'll cherish it."

He took her hands between his own and squeezed them lightly. Then he raised an arm and waited for the crowd to quiet. He thanked them all for sharing the special day. He slid an arm around Lorette's shoulders and looked down at her. "And I thank God for bringing the gift of Lorette into my life."

Lorette's heart stumbled. He seemed so sincere. She wanted to believe he thought her a gift, but it felt like trusting in daydreams. Hadn't she given up the dream of marrying a man who loved her?

The ride back to the farm wasn't nearly long enough, Lorette felt. Chase had explained that as a bachelor, he hadn't put time and money into building a 'real' house yet. He lived in a one-room soddy. They had agreed it was best to live in Tom and Bess's home.

She was trembling when he helped her

down from the wagon. He kept his hands lightly on her waist. She didn't dare lift her gaze to his but stared into his shoulder.

"If you want, I can spend the night at my soddy."

She shook her head. "No," she whispered. What if the neighbors spotted him heading to Bess and Tom's from his own place in the morning? It would be terribly embarrassing.

He bent his head and touched his lips to hers, quickly and lightly. Slowly his arms slid around her waist, drawing her closer. Her heart tripped over itself. He kissed her again, his lips soft, lingering, questioning, sweeter than she'd imagined a kiss could be.

Lorette wanted to abandon herself to his arms and kisses, but her chest burned. How could she give herself freely when he hadn't said he loved her? She pushed lightly against his shoulders.

He pulled his lips from hers immediately and rested his head against hers. His breath was coming quickly and unevenly. They stood that way for many minutes, until they heard Samuel fussing in his makeshift bed in the back of the wagon.

Lorette felt cold when Chase released her to pick up the boy. He placed Samuel in Lorette's arms. "I'll put Boots away while you put Sam to bed."

She nodded and started up the porch steps. Her heart hammered in her ears. What would happen when Chase came inside? Would he expect . . .

"Lorette."

She couldn't see his features as he stood in the late evening shadows beside Boots.

"It's all right, Lorette." His voice was gentle. "I'll sleep in one of the other rooms."

Lorette wasn't sure whether she felt relief or regret as she carried Samuel up to her bedchamber.

Chapter 7

The first few days after their marriage, things felt strained to Lorette between herself and Chase. Marriage hadn't changed their daily lives much. Chase had been an integral part of her life and Samuel's before the marriage; now they just lived under the same roof.

That they no longer referred to each other as Mr. Lankford and Miss Taber, but as Chase and Lorette, was only a symbol of the true changes. Her emotions were vulnerable in a new and terrifying way. She was self-conscious about every look between them, every casual touch. Her life and Samuel's were no longer hers alone to control. She was tied to Chase and this land forever.

One rainy evening in late July Chase took a fussy Samuel into the family room while Lorette cleaned up after the meal. She shaved soap into the enamel dishpan and poured in hot water from the steaming teakettle. Setting the kettle back on the stove, she paused at the sound of Chase's deep voice singing a lullaby.

Smiling, she tiptoed to the doorway and peeked in. Chase was seated in Bess's tapestry covered rocker, dwarfing the delicate chair. He didn't notice her. His attention was on Samuel lying on his lap in total trust, his eyes closed. The hominess of the scene was endearing.

When Chase finished the simple melody for the third time, she cleared her throat to get his attention. He looked up with a silly grin that showed her he was embarrassed.

Not wanting to awaken Samuel, she walked softly until she was close enough to whisper. "My mother sang that to Bess and me when we were little."

"Tell me about your childhood."

She lowered herself to the small crewel-covered footstool and told of growing up in Philadelphia. It had been a happy life until her parents were killed in a train accident. Soon after, she'd found a position as a governess, and Bess married Tom and moved to the Minnesota prairie.

Inclement weather made the room darker than usual for the hour, and Lorette hadn't lit the lamps yet. Perhaps the atmosphere made it easier for them to confide in each other in new ways.

Chase told her about his own life, his early childhood years in the East, coming west to Wisconsin with his parents to farm, then moving here to homestead as a young man. He hadn't as much land under acreage as Tom. He'd begun assisting Tom for money, working his own land at the same time. It was a long, hard road, but Chase didn't mind.

"Tom used to talk about when Sam and Aaron would be old enough to work beside him in the fields. He hoped to eventually buy more land so he could help them get started on their own farms."

"Bess spoke of that, too, in her journals." *I made the right decision, marrying Chase,* Lorette thought. *He understands and shares Bess and Tom's dreams for Samuel. It's obvious he loves the boy.*

"By the time Sam is grown and claims his inheritance, we'll have a real house on our land."

This was the first time either of them had spoken of their distant future together,

96

when it would be just the two of them in a marriage without the boy who had brought them together. She'd been too busy with everyday life to consider that such a time might come. The thought was a disturbing one to Lorette. "I'd best get back to the dishes before the water gets cold."

His words stayed with her. "*We* will have a real house on *our* land."

Always in the back of her mind she'd wondered whether Bess and Tom's land and their new house had been important factors behind Chase's proposal. The way he spoke tonight, it didn't appear so. "*We* will have a real house on *our* land." His words seemed filled with promise, as though he believed one day their marriage would be beautiful and rich in its normalness.

For days his words came back to her at odd times while she played with Samuel, or cared for the animals, or worked about the house. Weeding in the garden two weeks later the picture of Chase rocking Samuel and singing the lullaby filled her mind. "Oh, my!" Her hands stilled the hoe as a surprising and dismaying thought struck.

"This is the life I wished for when I was back in Philadelphia," she told an uncomprehending Samuel, who sat in the dirt happily yanking at a stubborn weed.

Wonder filled her at the realization. She hadn't wished to be a farm wife, she thought, placing a hand on her lower back and stretching stiff muscles. But she'd wished for her own family. Bess's letters, which had bubbled over with love for Tom and the children, had stirred embers of envy in Lorette's heart.

"Now I have my own family — and all because Bess and Tom died." She looked across the land to where the crosses were barely visible through wind-whipped prairie grass. She didn't believe God allowed Bess and Tom to die in order to give Lorette a ready-made family. But living on the prairie, she saw that nature and God waste nothing, even death. In one way or another all death brought new life out here.

Her gaze dropped to Samuel. "No!" She darted to him, bending over and pulling his hand from his mouth. She opened the sticky, dirty fingers and removed a granite colored stone with a sigh of relief. "I have to watch you every minute."

"Uh! Uh!" He made grasping motions with his fingers.

"No."

Samuel struggled to his feet and started down the row, trying out his new-found independence in walking. Three steps along he tumbled into the dirt. Curly, who was never far away when Lorette was outside with Samuel, stuck his nose in Samuel's face to be sure he was okay. Samuel pushed himself up on his forearms and shook his head until his curls shook, too. "No. No, Da."

Lorette laughed. Samuel's vocabulary only included four words: mama, papa, no, and da for dog. Sometimes he called her mama and Chase papa. It was hard to hear. She and Chase agreed Samuel would always know who his parents were, but he wasn't old enough to understand yet.

She took his hand as he struggled to his feet. "Let's go back to the house and get dinner ready."

Contentment filled her as they walked slowly along with his little fingers clutching hers. Every few steps he'd fight for balance, sometimes winning, sometimes losing. "You're getting better at walking every day," she told him.

Like she and Chase and Samuel were getting better at being a family every day. She knew Chase loved Samuel. She was pretty sure Chase liked her. But liking wasn't loving. *That's the part of my dream that's missing,* she thought, her heart twisting, *a husband who loves me.*

Lorette stole a moment to look out Kari Bresven's kitchen window at the late summer fields bathed in sunshine. The crops were abundant and beautiful, but they wouldn't be standing long. Harvest was going well. Chase, like most of the area farmers, had hired men to help. The neighbors were helping each other out, too. Harvest on Chase and Lorette's crops had been completed yesterday. Today Chase was helping in the Bresvens' fields, and Lorette and other neighbor women were helping Kari in the kitchen as the women had helped Lorette previously. Kari's children watched Samuel and some of the other wives' young ones so the women could work unimpeded.

Throughout the last week Lorette had fried chicken, peeled potatoes, and baked ten loaves of bread and a dozen pies. Now she was peeling potatoes again and wondering whether she would have any skin left on her fingers after harvest.

"Watching for a glimpse of that good-looking husband of yours?" a voice teased behind her.

Lorette turned with a smile but ignored the jest. "Catching a bit of breeze." She liked Susan, a dark-haired young farm wife. Lorette thought Susan seemed much younger and more carefree than herself, though she was only a year younger and had been married five years.

Lorette stepped back to the worktable and glanced in dismay at the pile of un-peeled potatoes on which she and Susan were working. It looked like it had grown in the few seconds she'd spent at the window. Already she missed the breeze. She'd grown accustomed to the prairie winds. They were quieter than usual today, and the house was hot from the oven that had been going since before dawn. The smell of fresh-baked bread and pies didn't make the heat any easier to bear. Her dress stuck to her and her hair itched.

Susan finished peeling another potato and continued her teasing. "A number of young ladies had their bonnets set for your husband when he was single."

Lorette glanced at her in surprise. Un-married men greatly outnumbered unmar-ried women in the area. Why hadn't it occurred to her to wonder before why Chase, who loved children and family, hadn't married before she came along?

"Good thing he waited." Kari set a kettle of cold water on the table for the peeled potatoes.

Lorette began to feel uneasy with the turn in conversation. The women were talking as if they didn't remember the rumors that precipitated Chase's proposal. She shifted her worried gaze to Kari.

The practical woman said quietly, "I've known Chase a long time. It's easy to see you make him happy."

Her words warmed Lorette's heart. She knew the hasty wedding hadn't fooled Kari, but the dear woman believed she and Chase could make a happy marriage even with such a beginning.

"He's not as good-looking as my husband of course," Susan continued with a laugh, "but he's a good man."

Lorette smiled. "Yes."

Kari brushed her hands down her apron. "There's nothing wrong with Chase Lankford's looks that I can see."

Susan shrugged good-naturedly. "I guess handsome is in the eye of the beholder."

Lorette shared in the laughter Susan's misquote brought. It was fun to be teased about Chase. She thought him by far the best looking man she'd seen since her arrival from Philadelphia, but it wouldn't have mattered if he was bald and had to bend over to see his boots. It was Chase's heart she loved.

Out in the yard, large pieces of wood were set on sawhorses and barrels to form a long table. At noon when the men came in from the fields Lorette watched eagerly for Chase while carrying food from the house to the table. They only shared quick smiles as they passed. Lorette enjoyed the visiting that went on with harvest time, but she missed the family meals with just her, Chase, and Samuel.

The table almost groaned under the heavy load of food. Lorette walked down one side filling coffee cups while the men loaded their plates. Each of the men had washed up at the pails of water on the back porch before sitting down, but it seemed to Lorette that the washing hadn't decreased the smell of sweat and kerosene one iota.

When she came to Chase he lifted his cup for her. "Things going all right this morning?"

She met his gaze, found him smiling into her eyes, and returned his smile. "Yes, fine. How are things going in the fields?"

He hadn't a chance to answer. Susan's husband, Ben, seated across from Chase, spoke first in a loud voice meant to draw attention. "Can sure tell yer a newlywed, Lankford. Come from a hot morning in the fields and yer more interested in speaking to yer wife than eating."

Ben's eyes sparkled with fun, but Lorette knew her cheeks flamed from his comments. She went on with her work.

Susan didn't ignore him. "Stop your teasing, Ben. Every man should look at his wife the way Chase looks at Lorette."

"Better listen up, Ben." Laughter threaded Chase's words.

Lorette darted a surprised look at Chase. He grinned at her in a manner that was downright flirtatious. Flustered, she murmured something about getting more coffee, though the pot still felt heavy, and retreated to the hot kitchen.

During the afternoon, Chase's looks and words danced through Lorette's mind. Ben's comments hadn't appeared to embarrass Chase at all. Still, she tried to avoid giving cause for further comments at the group supper and was glad when they finally left for home.

Chase brought in the large tin tub from the shed to the kitchen and Lorette heated water for their Saturday night baths while Chase took care of the animals. Samuel was the first to be bathed. Lorette had hoped the long day with the other children would have tired him, but it seemed to have energized him instead. She was glad Chase offered to watch the boy in the sitting room while she bathed.

The change into clean clothes felt good after the long hot day. She towel dried her hair and combed it out, letting it hang loose to dry.

When she entered the sitting room, Chase was holding Samuel and standing in front of Bess and Tom's family picture. Chase glanced at her. "Sam looks more like his father every day."

Lorette compared the boy to the image of the man. "Yes." Even in the lamplight the similarity was noticeable. So were the lines in Chase's face. He looked weary. She was sure he was wishing Tom and his family hadn't died. He would think it no use saying so; his wishing wouldn't bring them back.

Samuel wriggled and pushed at Chase's chest, and Chase set him down.

"I'll watch him now," Lorette said.

"He's mighty full of life for so late. He's trying to climb up on everything, when he's not chewing it."

"I'll rock him and read to him. I read to him every day from Bess's journal. I like knowing he is hearing his mother's words, even if he doesn't know they are hers." She shrugged, self-conscious at her revelation, half expecting him to laugh.

Chase touched her cheek, brushing his thumb slowly and gently over it. "When he's older, I'll tell him you did this for him, and he'll read her journals himself."

His sweet intimacy was unexpected. He never touched her in such a personal manner. His understanding made it a moment she knew she would cherish. "Thank you," she whispered.

A frustrated grunt cut the moment off as effectively as a slamming door.

"No!" They hollered at the same time. Both lunged for Samuel. Chase reached the boy first, swinging him up with only an inch to spare before Samuel would have grabbed the fringed table covering beneath the fancy lit kerosene lamp.

Lorette was shaking when Chase put the boy into her arms. "Close call." Chase shook his head before heading for the kitchen and his bath.

Lorette had to rock the struggling youngster for a few minutes to calm herself before she could read. She and Samuel had read almost the entire journal; they were up to the last entry. Lorette looked at the date and a sadness welled up in her. The date was the day before Bess died.

Aaron and Liza are complaining of sore throats, and mine is feeling a bit scratchy. Such a time to come down with something, with Lorette coming in a couple days. I can barely contain my excitement at seeing her again! I keep thinking of things I must tell her, and must ask her, and memories I want to relive with her. I do hope she will be happy working for the Henrys, though I confess another fantasy has crossed my mind a few times since she agreed to come out west. I like to pretend she and Chase fall in love . . .

Lorette's voice stumbled. She glanced at the closed kitchen door. Had Chase heard? She lowered her words to barely a whisper.

I like to pretend she and Chase fall in love and marry. Tom tells me to quit being fanciful, but it would be such fun to have my sister and Tom's best friend for neighbors. Our children could grow up together.

She closed the book. "That's your

mother's last entry, Samuel."

He plopped both hands on the leather cover. "Mama."

Tears leaped to her eyes and she hugged him close. "Yes."

The door opened and Chase stuck his wet head into the room. "I'm going out to check on the animals one last time." A moment later she heard the outside door squeak open and close again.

In a shaky voice, she began singing a lullaby. After what seemed a long time, Samuel fell asleep. She placed him in his crib and went to stand on the porch.

The weather was pleasant, having cooled off after the sun went down. An orange harvest moon brightened the landscape. In the pale light she saw Chase walking back from the graves.

"I was thinking," he said when he arrived at the porch, "that we should use some of the money from the crops to buy headstones."

Gratitude flooded her. "I'd like that. You were wonderful to make the crosses, but . . ."

"They aren't permanent like a headstone."

"No."

He came to stand beside her, leaning

against the rail and looking out over the land.

"I'm going to miss the crops," she told him. "I liked watching them grow and change. As they grew they changed the landscape. Sometimes the colors changed from hour to hour, depending on the height of the sun, and the movement of the clouds, or the wiles of the winds."

He chuckled. "They'll be back next year."

Lorette looked down at the wooden rail and ran her fingers lightly along it. Her heart beat hard against her chest as she built up her courage to ask the question she'd been wondering about since morning. "Why didn't you marry before you met me?"

He was silent so long that she finally looked at him. His face looked taut in the shadows cast by the moon.

"Never mind. I shouldn't have asked."

He took a deep breath. "You have every right to ask. You're my wife. You can ask me anything."

Lorette tried to drink in the wonder of his words before he continued.

"I'd been courting a girl when I decided to move out here and homestead. Thought I loved her. Thought she loved me, too.

When I told her my plans and asked her to marry me, she said she'd never marry a farmer."

Lorette didn't know what to say. She reached out and tentatively laid a hand on his forearm. He covered her hand with his own and went on with his story.

"Gave up on the idea of love and marriage after that. Then I met Tom and Bess. Tom, he sure was crazy in love with your sister. After awhile, seeing them together, I began to have second thoughts about getting married, but I didn't meet anyone I wanted to spend my life with." He squeezed her hand. "Then God brought you into my life."

Her throat tightened. Was he saying he truly cared for her?

"I saw the sacrifices you were making for Samuel, the hard life you took on without a whimper of self-pity. Every day I found myself liking you more, and then it was more than liking."

Lorette could barely breathe. Was he saying he loved her?

He slid his hand from hers, and her fingers felt suddenly cool in the night air. "It was wrong to ask you to marry me the way I did." His voice sounded hard.

"Wh . . . why?"

"You were grieving for Bess and you'd just found out about the rumors. No one could be expected to think clearly about what they want and need at such a time." He shoved both hands through his hair and turned to her. "I was so terrified you might move back East that I was glad for an excuse to press you to marry me. But maybe I've ruined your life. Maybe you would have been happier back East, and now I've tied you to me and to this land."

He'd wanted to marry her for herself, not only for Samuel! Joy flooded her at the realization, but he still hadn't said he loved her. She chose her words carefully.

"I'm beginning to understand Bess's love for this land. When I first came here, I thought the prairie was a threatening place. Living on the farm has made me aware of nature's life, death, life cycle. I'll never stop missing Bess, but I'm able to accept her death better now. I realize the land isn't the enemy. We aren't in battle against it. We're in partnership with it." Lorette could feel his gaze on her.

"We?" His tone was wary.

Lorette met his gaze. "I've no desire to move back East. Every day when you leave for the fields or chores, it seems all Samuel and I do is wait for you to return."

His hands lifted slowly and framed her face. "I love you, Lorette. I've loved you almost since you moved out to the farm, but I didn't think you'd want to hear it."

"I do want to hear it. I want to hear it every day."

He pulled her into his arms and whispered against her hair, "I love you, Lorette. I love you. I love you."

She relaxed against him, drinking in the words she'd waited so long to hear. "I love you, too," she replied shyly, whispering the words she'd been waiting all her life to say.

He chuckled, lifting her in his arms and swinging her around in a circle again and again, his boots thunking against the porch boards. "I want to hear it every day, too," he demanded.

He kissed her soundly on the lips, his arms tight about her waist, then lowered her slowly until she stood on her own feet. His kisses didn't stop. They grew sweeter and lingered longer and longer and longer.

"I should get you inside before it gets too cool out here," Chase finally said.

Lorette nodded against his shoulder. Her last thought as they walked into their home wrapped in each other's arms was that the Lord had indeed made a way for her and Samuel; He'd made a very nice way indeed.

A Vow
Unbroken

by Amy Rognlie

Prologue

Abby Cantrell stared at the date at the top of the letter, her eyes widening.

April 29, 1881. Why hadn't Aunt Caroline told her it would be so soon? Dropping down into the chair, she smoothed the crisp paper, reading again the telltale words.

Dear Miss Peters,

I can't tell you how happy I was to receive your letter this past week. I trust that you, as do I, look forward to the approaching day when we shall meet here in Littleton. Enclosed is the train ticket, as well as a little extra money in case you have need of something. I will be waiting for you on the appointed day. Until then, I re-main yours truly,

James Parrish

Abby jumped as footsteps sounded in the tiled hallway. Slipping the letter back into the Bible where she had found it, she stood and ambled over to the library window. The fading sunset cast shadows on the budding trees, holding her gaze until she heard the footsteps behind her, their sound muffled by the plush carpet.

"Beautiful evening."

The softly spoken words invaded the tumult in Abby's mind. She sighed, turning slightly to drape her arm over the shoulders of the small woman beside her. The comforting scent of roses embraced her. "What am I going to do, Mama?"

Hazel Peters smoothed her daughter's dark hair. "I don't know, dear. Surely God has a plan. . . ." She fell silent as Abby turned away to gaze out of the lace-framed window. The silence stretched, broken only by the sound of the mourning doves getting ready to roost. "But I do know this," Hazel whispered. "He said He would not give us more than we could bear."

Abby eyed the darkening sky. Her mind acknowledged the truth of her mother's words, but her heart felt the shadows of night moving slowly and surely, threatening to plunge her into a darkness unlike any she had ever known.

Chapter 1

James Parrish gripped his cap tightly at the sound of a distant train whistle. He scarcely noticed the porters checking the luggage or the scampering children. His concentrations focused upon the tiny, moving speck in the distance. Perspiration prickled at the nape of his neck.

Would she be on the train, as she had promised? He had waited so long, had poured over her letter, had dreamed of what she would look like. *Miss Caroline Peters.* He liked the sound of it as he rolled it around in his mind. He stared at the train, now close enough for him to read the letters on the side. The Denver Rio Grand Railway. He peered anxiously at the windows, straining to see as the train squealed to a stop. Was she finally here?

He watched the passengers as they disembarked. Most were Denverites coming to Littleton for a day in the country. He kneaded his cap, his eyes locked on the straggling line of people. There. Was that her? His heart leapt as he spied a dark-haired woman coming toward him, a welcoming smile on her lovely face. She had almost reached him, when an older gentleman brushed past him and grasped her arm.

James exhaled forcefully and turned his attention back to those still struggling down the narrow steps, their valises bumping their sides. He wished that he had a more detailed description, but the brief one she had sent him would have to do. He would find her, if it was the last thing . . . wait. There. That had to be her. One of the last passengers to come down the steps, she paused at the platform as if unsure of herself. He watched her glance about, the fetching pink feather in her hat softly dancing, her arms full. He couldn't see her face very well, until her gaze fell on him.

The woman smiled tentatively and he started toward her as if in a dream, his gaze locked with hers. Finally, he stood in front of her. Her hazel eyes reminded him of the first greening of spring. She was beautiful. And so small. She barely came up to his shoulder. . . .

"Mr. Parrish?" At her softly spoken words, James realized that he had been staring.

"Yes, I'm Mr. Parrish." He winced at how stiff and formal he sounded. He had wanted to greet her warmly. Welcoming. But meeting this way was just so awkward.

"I'm glad to finally be here. And to make your acquaintance," she said.

Her voice sounded weary, and as James continued to study her face, he noted the purple shadows under those beautiful eyes. Her journey had been a long one, he realized. But did her eyes reflect more than weariness? Sorrow, perhaps?

He watched her out of the corner of his eye as he collected her trunk. She was so beautiful; he could scarcely believe it. Of course, he had made up his mind that he would love his new bride, no matter what she looked like. Yet, the Lord had chosen to bless him with a beauty of a wife. He smiled at her tenderly, then offered his hand to help her into the wagon. For the first time, he found himself wishing he had a nice carriage. Still, she knew he was a farmer. Surely she hadn't expected anything fancy.

He watched her gather her skirts to climb into the wagon. As she leaned into his grip to hoist herself up, her foot slipped. Instinctively, he caught her as she fell backward, catching a whiff of her perfume as well. He set her carefully on her feet, his heart pounding at her nearness. He wanted to hold her in his arms and never let her go.

She stammered out an apology, bending laboriously to retrieve her shawl from the dusty street. Straightening up, she met his shocked gaze. She was with child!

Dear God, what kind of cruel trick has this woman played on me? He gaped at her in silence. *How could she?*

Vulnerability briefly shimmered in her eyes before a glaze of weary resignation replaced it. "I suppose she didn't tell you."

"Who?" he croaked.

She raised her eyebrows.

"Who didn't tell me what?" He swallowed against the sudden dryness in his throat, trying to gather his thoughts and steel himself for whatever explanation she would offer.

"My . . . aunt . . . Caroline . . ." Her shoulders drooped and tears filled her eyes, threatening to spill over.

James reached out to her instinctively, as he would to a forlorn child. He put his hand under her chin, marveling at how soft her skin was against the roughness of his own. "It's all right," he whispered. "Can you just explain . . . I mean . . . I . . . don't understand."

She swallowed hard but didn't pull away from his touch. "My aunt Caroline. She didn't tell you that I was in the family way." Her words formed a statement rather than a question.

Silence settled between them as James struggled to comprehend her words. Why had Caroline's pregnant niece come, and not Caroline? Were they trying to trick him? If so, why? Was this all a big joke on him — the dumb farmer out in cow country? The heat began to rise in his face. How could he have been so idealistic — so hopefully stupid — to believe that he would finally have wife?

He glanced back down at her, his mental tirade ceasing when he met the misery in her eyes.

"I'm so sorry," she whispered. "She said she didn't think you'd mind if I came in her place. She . . . I should have known she wouldn't have told you. But I can still work. I'll do anything you need me to do. I don't know how to do anything on a farm, but I can cook and clean, and . . ."

Her words trailed off as he scrutinized her. He couldn't believe someone so small could carry such a large child. He doubted she'd be doing much cooking and cleaning for quite awhile. He shook his head in disbelief at this bewildering situation. "If you are not Miss Caroline, then I suppose I don't even know your name."

"Abigail Cantrell." She gave him a faint smile. "Most people call me Abby."

What else should he say? "Well, Abby . . ."

Her face clouded. "I guess I'm just not what you were expecting, Mr. Parrish. I'm so sorry. . . ."

He made an effort to grin, but failed. "Can I ask you . . . why Caroline didn't come?" Did she decide that life on a farm would be too dull, so she sent her niece instead?

Abby looked pained. "It's a long story, Mr. Parrish. However, I assure your arrangement wouldn't have worked out anyway. Caroline is . . . would not be suited for the work."

Why does she keep talking about all the hard work? Sure, it is work to be a farmer's wife, but that's not the reason I searched for a wife. Only God knows how long I've yearned for a companion, someone to share life's sorrows and joys. James cleared his throat, hoping for some inspiration to seize him. What was he supposed to do with a pregnant woman? He couldn't very well marry her now, could he? But, what else . . . ?

"Might there be somewhere I could get a drink of water?" she asked.

Abby's soft voice pulled his attention back to her. The look of utter exhaustion on her face smote his heart with regret. How long had he kept her standing outside in the blazing sun, and in her condition? "Forgive me," he said, giving her his hand.

She sighed with relief as she sank down onto the wagon seat, closing her eyes as if she would fall asleep right there. James clucked to the horses then glanced at her in concern. "Are you all right, ma'am?"

Guiltily, her eyes popped open. "I didn't sleep very well on the train, I guess." She gazed at him. "How far do you live from town?"

James swallowed hard, feeling slightly addled. *Surely she doesn't think I am going to marry her!* "Uh, not too far. I hadn't planned on us going home until tomorrow . . . but I guess . . ."

She bit her lip, obviously sensing his turmoil. "It's all right, Mr. Parrish. I should have known. . . ." She straightened her shoulders. "I don't want you to feel beholden to me. If you'll just let me off at a boardinghouse, I'm sure I can find some other work."

He gaped at her. What kind of man did she think he was? True, she didn't know a thing about him. But, surely she didn't think that he would just dump her in a strange town. He was responsible for bringing her here, wasn't he? "I can't do that, ma'am," he said softly. "I'm sure we can work something out."

The relief in her eyes spoke volumes. After all, what kind of "work" could she find in her condition? The thought made him cringe.

"I'm a good cook," she offered timidly.

He smiled then, his first real smile since this peculiar situation began. "Well, I like to eat. So I guess we're off to a good start." *But what do I do now?* He glanced at her small, glove-covered hands clasped demurely in her lap. Or what was left of her lap.

"When is . . . I mean how long until . . ." He felt his face redden at his clumsy questioning.

"The child will be born in about six weeks, Mr. Parrish." She didn't smile, but he thought he detected a glint of humor in her large eyes.

"Ah, I see. Well . . . I . . ." *Dear Lord, help me,* he pleaded silently. *I'm in over my head, and I don't know what to do.*

The voice in his heart replied, *Show her the way to Me.*

James swallowed hard, then made up his mind. "Ma'am, I know that you're very tired. I'm going to take you to the boardinghouse, and we can talk more in the morning."

"Thank you," she said, giving him a small smile.

They drove the rest of the short distance in silence. James pulled up in front of his sister's house, jumping off the wagon seat as soon as the horses came to a halt. Abby was looking paler by the minute. Lifting her gingerly down from the wagon, he escorted her to Iris's door. "Hope you got a room ready, Sis," he hollered in through the screen door.

Iris came running, her eyes widening as she took in the couple standing on her porch. Her gaze flew to James's face. He frowned slightly and shook his head, and she nodded, turning her attention to Abby.

"You look worn out, dear. Come in and let me fix you a cup of tea."

James silently blessed his sister for not questioning him. He released Abby into her care with a sigh of relief. "Miss . . . uh, ma'am, this is my sister Iris." He pasted a smile on his face. "I'll be back in the morning, ladies." Turning, he strode back to the wagon as fast as he could without actually running. What kind of a mess had he gotten himself into?

Chapter 2

Abby stared after him for a long moment, wondering what was going through his mind. He had seemed to be such a gentleman, although she was obviously not what he had expected. What in the world had Caroline told the poor man?

He was a lot younger than Abby had expected. *Yes, quite a bit younger,* she mused. *And handsome, too. With hair the color of sun-kissed wheat, eyes —*

"Come on in, dear," Iris repeated, breaking into Abby's wandering thoughts. "I guess James forgot to tell me your name."

Abby looked up to find Iris's brilliant eyes, eyes the same bright blue as her brother's, fastened on her face. "Abby

Cantrell. I'm so sorry. . . ."

"Nonsense." Iris gave an unladylike snort, accompanied by a friendly grin. "You're tired from your long trip, and James brought you here so you could rest. That's no reason to be sorry."

Abby sighed as she slogged into the house after Iris, feeling as if she might collapse if she remained on her feet much longer.

"Now, you just sit down here and put your feet up on this stool," Iris commanded. "I'll bring you a cup of tea."

Abby obeyed, her heart warming at the genuine friendliness of the woman.

Iris reappeared with two steaming cups. Handing one to Abby, she settled herself comfortably on a floral tapestry settee. "Now, tell me all about yourself, Abby."

James clenched his teeth against the jarring of the wagon as it bumped over the dirt road. How could the day's events have taken such an unexpected turn? He sighed as he pulled up in front of the farmhouse. He should have been bringing a bride home. But, instead of a bride, he had a problem. A big one.

He did his chores mechanically, then sank down in his favorite rocker in front of the hearth. Since she — no, since Caroline — answered his newspaper advertisement, he had dreamed of his bride sitting next to him in this very room, sharing treasured moments from the day, just being together. Now that's all it was — a dream.

God, I thought you were leading me. I thought I was doing Your will. He pictured Abby's face. She was all he had hoped for in a wife. Even in the short time he was with her, he could sense her gentle spirit. And she was beautiful, too, of course.

But what of the child? He wished he'd had the presence of mind to ask her more questions. How could she possibly even think that he would marry her? It wasn't just the fact that she was carrying a child, but that he felt somehow deceived. Had it been their plan all along? Was she running from some sort of trouble? *Maybe her family sent her away when they learned the shameful truth of what she had done — or had done to her,* he thought.

He felt his head begin to throb. What did she want from him? A sudden horrifying thought came to him. What if there really was no Aunt Caroline, and what if Abby was already married? Maybe she was running away from her husband. He had heard of such things happening. But then . . . he thought again of the wounded look in her expressive eyes, her shy smile, the way she carried herself with womanly dignity, and he couldn't believe anything sordid about her.

"Well, Lord, I guess You will have to show me what to do with this young lady," he said aloud. "All I know is, I prayed long and fervently for a wife . . . and Abby Cantrell is the one that arrived on the train." He picked up his well-worn Bible from the hearth. "If she's the one You sent me, I need to know."

"Lean not unto thine own understanding. In all thy ways acknowledge him, and he shall direct thy paths." The oft-read verse from Proverbs jumped out at him. He closed his eyes, remembering the still, small voice that had spoken earlier.

Show her the way to Me. Show her the way to Me.

After a long while, James rose and went to bed. Tomorrow should prove to be a day he would remember for years to come — his wedding day.

His heart began a slow thump when he saw her sitting on Iris's porch steps, the morning sun glinting off her dark, shiny hair. She smiled at him, and he couldn't seem to remember anything he had planned to say.

He swiped his hat off as he neared the porch. "Good morning, ma'am. Did you sleep well?"

She nodded. "Yes, thank you."

He gestured to the step. "May I?" At her nod, he seated himself next to her, immediately assailed with her scent that he remembered vividly from yesterday, from that brief intoxicating moment he had held her in his arms. She smelled like a sun-drenched field of wildflowers. He scooted a little farther away, trying to regain his train of thought. "I, uh, thought we'd better discuss a few things," he said, feeling like an awkward schoolboy.

She darted an amused glance at him. "I'm not going to bite you, Mr. Parrish."

He grinned sheepishly, fascinated with the way her hazel eyes were smiling at him. "I've decided that we can still get married," he blurted.

Her mouth dropped open. "M–married?"

What is going on here? Surely she —

"Isn't that why you came here?" he asked cautiously.

She stared at him wordlessly for a long minute. "I . . . no. I did not come here to

132

get married. Caroline told me . . ." Her voice trailed off, and her gaze turned compassionate. "That's why you were so disappointed when you saw me."

Disappointed? That wasn't the word I would have chosen.

"No, no," he said hastily. "Not disappointed. Just . . . surprised."

She didn't look convinced.

"I just never imagined —" He stopped as he noticed her lips beginning to twitch. Was she . . . laughing? He smiled into her eyes, a chuckle working its way up to his throat. "I guess it is kind of funny," he said.

She glanced back down at her protruding belly, but not before a soft giggle escaped. "Forgive me. It's just that —" She giggled again, and this time he laughed with her. Soon they were shaking with laughter, tears running down their faces.

He finally caught his breath. "Perhaps we should introduce ourselves all over again," he suggested.

She dabbed at her eyes with a lacy handkerchief. "All right." Her eyes still danced with laughter as she gave him her hand. "I'm Abigail Cantrell, your new housekeeper."

He bowed over her hand then captured

her gaze with his. "Pleased to meet you, Abigail Cantrell. I am James Parrish, your future husband."

The light in her eyes dimmed, and he felt her small hand tremble beneath his. "I'm not so sure that's such a good idea, Mr. Parrish. You see, I'm not a free woman."

She felt him start. "I wasn't going to tell you all this, but I guess I owe it to you." She gently withdrew her hand from his. "I suppose you'll put me back on the train once you hear my story." It had taken all the courage she possessed just to leave home and all she had known to come west. And now —

He shook his head. "I don't think so."

She moved restlessly, feeling the weight of the babe in her womb, and the still greater weight of her guilt bearing down on her. Why, oh why had she gone against Papa so willfully? Then none of this would have happened. She would still be enjoying the peaceful life she had always known.

She finally remembered the silent man sitting next to her, and she turned to gaze at him. Why couldn't she have met someone like James before — ? She noticed the tiny laugh lines around his eyes and the gentle peace written there, drawing her like a magnet. Something deep within her reached out to him, as it had from the first moment they had met.

He watched her quietly as she studied him, and suddenly she knew that she could trust him with her life. "I'm not sure where to begin," she said, searching his blue eyes again, just to make sure. "I guess I should tell you that I'm widowed."

He nodded, an unreadable expression on his face.

"My husband died six months ago." Her flat, emotionless voice matched her feelings. "We were just suspecting my condition at the time of his death." Shifting her weight, Abby tried unsuccessfully to find a comfortable position on the hard porch step.

"But if the truth be told, I don't regret the fact that Charles never knew about our child. You see, when my husband died, I learned that he wasn't the man I thought he was. . . ."

James frowned. "I'm afraid I don't understand."

She smiled ruefully. "I'm not sure I do, either, Mr. Parrish. And I'm not sure I'm up to explaining it all to you now. Perhaps some other day. But, suffice to say, my husband . . ." She stumbled over the word, then began again. "My husband was involved in something . . . unlawful."

"And so?"

Abby raised her eyebrows, wondering why he hadn't made the obvious connection. How could she make it plainer? "My husband committed some crimes. Then he died. Someone has to pay for what he did."

He frowned again. "Pardon me for saying so, ma'am, but as much as I know about the law, I don't think that a widow is expected to be punished for her husband's crimes."

"Oh no. Not the law." She took a deep breath. "It's God that I'm concerned about."

"God? But God doesn't require —"

"I, too, did some things that I regret. And so I made a vow to God, Mr. Parrish, the day that Charles died. It cannot be broken." She could see the shock written on his face, but she plunged ahead, wanting to get it over with. "I will not allow someone else to be hurt because of my sins." It sounded so stark, so melodramatic. But it was the truth.

"And the vow was?" His voice was grave, his gaze unwavering.

The question reverberated in the quiet morning air, a cricket chirping under the porch the only sound for a long minute.

She closed her eyes briefly, then opened them to look directly into his. "I have vowed that I will never love anyone again."

James took in the earnestness of her sweet face, and his heart ached for her. How had she missed the fact that love is the very essence of God? How could she think that a loving God would want her to live life without love?

He gently reached for her hand, holding it firmly between both of his. "Abby, I would be honored if you would accept my hand in marriage."

She stared at him as if he had suddenly gone daft. "But I just told you —"

"You didn't promise God that you would never let anyone love you, did you?"

She dropped her gaze, but not before he saw the blush that colored her smooth cheeks. "No," she whispered.

"Then there's no problem. You need someone to love and care for you and your child." He smiled. "And I've been praying that God would send me a wife who I could love forever."

She met his gaze for an instant before staring down at her swollen belly again. "But I wouldn't be your wife . . . really."

He felt the back of his neck grow hot at the thought of it. He couldn't deny that he wanted her to be his wife in the fullest sense of the word, but until she was ready for that . . . "Look at me, Abby," he commanded gently.

He waited until she lifted uncertain eyes to his. "I promise you that I will take care of you and your baby to the best of my ability. I will honor you, and I promise you that I will never take advantage of you."

She swallowed hard. "Why?"

Why? Because I love you already, he thought, wishing he could take her in his arms and show her. "Because I asked God for a wife and he sent you, Abby."

"I don't deserve someone like you."

Her words were whispered, but the force of them nearly took his breath away.

God, please shine your grace on Abby, he prayed silently. *She's like a lost little girl.* "We all deserve to be loved, Abby."

"Are you sure?" A tiny spark of hope glinted in her eyes. "A lifetime is a long time, you know."

Long enough to convince you of my love. And long enough for you to return my love. He squeezed her hand. "I'm sure."

She gave him a small smile. "I hope you like my cooking."

An hour later, they stood in front of the justice of the peace. Iris had picked a huge bouquet of wildflowers, and Abby held them tightly now in her shaking hands. James stood beside her, his hand warm on the small of her back. "Just a few more minutes, Abby. Then we can go home," he whispered in her ear. She looked like she was about ready to keel over in exhaustion. Yet to James, she was the most beautiful bride he had ever seen. A shaft of late afternoon sunlight found its way into the dim parlor, illuminating her delicate face. Though some might say he was getting a bad deal, he confidently believed that this woman would hold his heart for eternity.

Chapter 3

"Well, this is the old homestead," James said.

Abby allowed him to help her down from the wagon, then gazed at the farmhouse appreciatively. It wasn't very big, but the place looked tidy and snug. Newly whitewashed and the wide front porch swept clean, her new home was a welcoming sight. She smiled up at him. "It's very nice, James." It still felt awkward to call him James instead of Mr. Parrish, but he was her husband, after all.

Could it have only been yesterday that she had arrived on the train from New York? Now, here she was — a newlywed. She still felt slightly stunned at the events of the last few hours. Yet, somehow, she was at peace.

It wouldn't be hard to live with James,

she decided, watching as he hefted her trunk out of the back of the wagon. She had never met a more caring, gentle man. Before she could pull her satchel from the wagon seat, James took the bag, then led her down the well-worn path toward the house. In pleasant surprise, Abby stopped by the front porch. The sweet-spicy fragrance of a beautiful pink rose in full bloom enchanted her.

"Do you like roses?"

James's low voice broke into her thoughts as she bent slightly to sniff a large blossom.

"This is exquisite." She glanced up at him, then swept the arid landscape with questioning eyes. "Wherever did you get a rose bush way out here?"

He shrugged. "I have friends who just made a trip back East. Had them bring it back for me." He smiled down at her. "I thought my new wife might like something pretty to welcome her."

Her eyes widened. What a thoughtful man! "How very kind . . . I don't know what to —" Her sentence ended in a shriek as something cold and wet pressed into her hand. She whirled around, her heart pounding as she came nose to nose with the largest dog she had ever seen. She backed up a step, her legs shaking.

Where had the dreadful creature come from? She cast a pleading glance at James. "Can you get it away from me?"

He chuckled, reaching for the dog's collar. "Sit, Frank," he commanded.

Abby sighed in relief, sinking down onto the porch steps. "Is that yours?" she asked.

James grinned. "Now, that's no way to talk about a family member, Abby," he drawled. "This is Frank. He's quite a feller."

"I'll say." Abby eyed the panting animal distrustfully. "So, he's a male dog?"

"Yep."

She swallowed hard, almost afraid to ask. "Does it . . . live in the house?"

James appeared to be trying not to laugh. "No. Frank is a farm dog." He scratched the dog's floppy ears. "Though he does sneak in at night every once in awhile when it's cold out."

"Oh." Abby peered at the dog again. Was he smirking at her? She didn't like the look in his eye. "I haven't been around dogs very much," she said.

"I kind of figured that." James plunked down next to her on the step. "But Frank won't hurt you. He likes you. See, just let him sniff your hand, like this." He reached out a hand, which Frank obligingly covered with dog kisses.

Be brave, Abby, she told herself. She reached her hand out toward the dog, stopping midway. "Why is it thumping its tail?" she whispered to James nervously. Maybe dogs thumped their tails right before they pounced on their prey.

James sighed, but she could still see the laughter in his eyes. "Frank is a he, not an it. And he's thumping his tail because he's happy."

"Oh." Abby folded her hands safely under her watermelon-sized stomach. "I'm very pleased to meet you, Frank," she said. "I'm sure we'll be friends," she added, fervently hoping that it would be so.

She glanced up at James, frowning. Why was the man making such strange noises?

The look on her face must have been the last straw, because his suppressed chuckles suddenly broke into hearty laughter.

"What is so funny?" she demanded. "All I said was —"

"I know!" James grinned. "I've just never heard such a polite speech to a dog!" He chuckled again. "I like you, Abby," he said, taking her hand.

She smiled back at him, her heart warming at his sincerity. "I like you, too, James," she said.

Frank gave a hearty woof and Abby jumped. She would have to get used to the creature, she supposed.

James pulled her to her feet, keeping her hand in his. "Come on, Mrs. Parrish. I'll show you through your new home."

It didn't take long for Abby to get settled. She hadn't brought many things with her, since she had thought she was coming to be a hired housekeeper. A few dresses, her Bible, and a few items she had sewn for the baby.

James sat watching her one night as she hemmed yet another tiny garment. "Is it a boy or a girl?" he asked.

She glanced up at him. "Only the good Lord knows that," she said. "But I like to think that my baby is a girl." She studied his face in the flickering light of the fire. "Why do you ask?"

He shrugged. "Just curious, I guess."

She smiled then turned her attention back to the soft white material.

He settled back in his rocker, watching her. She seemed happy enough, he thought, noticing the adorable way she held her lips in a slight pucker while she worked. He had memorized every line of her lovely face in the past few weeks, often watching her when she was unaware.

They had fallen into a comfortable routine. He would spend the days out in the wheat fields, while she tended the house and garden. She hadn't been exaggerating when she said she was a good cook. It was comforting to know that when he finished with his chores, she would be waiting for him with a smile and a delicious meal.

Yet, she had withdrawn from him since their wedding day. He had given her his bed, while he slept on a bedroll in front of the fire. She had seemed distressed that he had to sleep on the floor, he remembered with a smile. With such a kind and gentle spirit about her, how could anyone help but love her?

His eyes roamed to her stomach, and he watched in amusement as it moved with the baby's antics. He wondered if Abby were afraid. He had heard so many terrible stories about the travails of childbirth. Even his own mama . . . he sighed. They would simply have to face any problems should they come and trust the Lord to protect Abby when her time of delivery arrived. Stewing about tomorrow's problems would do no good.

In the meantime, he wanted to get to know Abby a little better. She seemed so remote since that first day when they had talked and laughed so easily. Oh, she was friendly, but aloof. Distant. He had hoped that at least they could be friends, even if they couldn't be lovers. He sighed again. Maybe he had been dreaming to think that this marriage, a marriage in name only, could really work.

Father, I was so sure I heard Your voice that day, he prayed inwardly. *Please show me what to do. I want to love Abby and care for her, but I feel like she regrets marrying me.*

Show her the way to Me. The still small voice echoed in his heart, reminding him of the first day they had met. Wasn't that what God had told him that first day? But how could he accomplish the task?

He glanced over at her bowed head. Her dark hair glinted in the light of the oil lamp beside her.

"Abby."

She looked up, her hands resting on her stomach. "Did you need something?"

Yes, I need you, he thought, his heart suddenly pounding. What he wouldn't give right now to have the right to take her in his arms. However, he must be patient. "I was wondering if you would like to have a time of prayer together in the evenings."

146

She looked surprised, and his heart sank. "I'd like that very much, James," she said quietly.

"You would?"

She nodded. "My mama and my sisters and I used to pray together every night. I've missed that since Charles and I . . . since . . . for a long time," she finished quickly.

One of these days he would ask her to tell him the whole story, James decided. But not right now. Reaching for his Bible, he laid it on his knees. "Would you like me to read anything in particular?"

She thought for a moment, her head tilted to one side. "I guess my favorite has always been the psalms," she said. "Maybe Psalm 91?"

"That's one of my favorites, too," he said, smiling into her eyes. In fact, he could have recited it from memory, but he lowered his gaze to the page, deciding it would be safer to read than to lose him in her large, hazel eyes.

" 'He that dwelleth in the secret place of the most High shall abide under the shadow of the Almighty. I will say of the Lord. . . .' " Before he was halfway through, he heard her reciting it softly with him. Closing the Bible with a soft thud, he laid it back down on the hearth then scooted his chair closer to hers. He reached for her hand, gently kissing her work-roughened fingertips before enfolding them in his grasp.

"Father God, Abby and I come before you tonight as your humble children. Lord, You have searched us and known us. You know our downsitting and our uprising and are acquainted with all our ways. There is not a word in our tongue, but Thou knowest it altogether. Thou hast beset us behind and before and laid Thine hand upon us. Such knowledge is too wonderful for us, it is high, and we cannot attain unto it. For where shall we go from Your presence? Where can we flee from Your spirit? Even if we take the wings of the morning and dwell in the uttermost part of the sea, even there shall You be. When we awake, we are still with Thee. Thank You, Father God, that by Your Holy Spirit, You are present with us always. Please teach me how to be a good husband to Abby, Father. Bless her and the child abundantly. We thank You, Father. In Jesus' name, Amen."

He raised his head, his heart too full for words, and saw the same written on his wife's face. And his soul rejoiced within him.

Chapter 4

Abby lay in bed, feeling her spirit moving within her as much as the child who kicked in her womb. She had never heard anyone pray like James had prayed tonight. Of course she recognized that he had borrowed a portion of his prayer from Psalm 139. Yet the way that he had prayed, with such assurance and fervor, amazed her. It had been so long since she had allowed herself to think of God as anything other than a tyrant. What used to be second nature now seemed unreal.

James was such a good person. She could tell from that very first day that she would face a constant battle to keep her vow. How easy it would be to love James, and let him love her. She couldn't help but notice the way his eyes followed her around the kitchen. And he always remembered to thank her for the meals she prepared.

"Mmph!" The baby gave a hard kick, and Abby grimaced. It was getting harder and harder to find a comfortable sleeping position. She rolled over on her side, trying to concentrate on the soothing smell of lavender that wafted from the fat bouquets she had hung in the attic to dry.

The fire had died down, but in the moonlight she could see enough to make out the features of James' face as he lay asleep on his bedroll. How many times had she caught herself in the last few days, just before she reached up to caress his cheek or to smooth his fair hair off of his forehead?

He was becoming dear to her. But that must not be. She would not allow it. If she started to love him, he would be taken away. Just like Papa. Just like Charles. Just like — she wrapped her arms around her stomach, hugging the babe to her in the cold night. No, she wouldn't even think it. Not her child, too. Even God wouldn't be so cruel, would He?

She squeezed her eyes shut against the pain and fear that threatened to overwhelm her. But her efforts did no good. The fear was like a living thing, threatening to squeeze the very breath out of her body.

"Abby! What's wrong?"

Her eyes flew open to see James standing over her. She must have cried out. She shook her head, taking a couple of deep breaths.

He sank down on his knees next to the bed and laid a cool hand on her forehead. "What is it, love?" he whispered. "Are you in pain? Is it the child?"

She shook her head again, tears welling up into her eyes. Swallowing against the lump in her throat, she grasped his hand and clung to it. Slowly the bands of fear loosened from around her chest.

"I'm sorry," she whispered. "It's just that sometimes I'm so afraid."

She felt him nod.

"Do you want me to sit with you for a while?" he whispered.

No, she wanted him to take her in his arms and hold her until she felt safe again. She wanted him to lie next to her, so she could feel protected. Loved. Secure. But that could never be. She was being weak to even let him sit near her and hold her hand.

She sighed. "I know you're tired. I'll be

fine." She thought, if he could have seen her face, he would have known she was lying.

He sat still for a few moments, then brushed his lips across her forehead. "He will never leave you nor forsake you, Abby," he whispered.

The outdoorsy smell of his warm skin lingered in her senses as he returned to his makeshift bed to lie back down. She squeezed her eyes shut against the lonely tears that seemed determined to fall. Surely morning would come soon.

Morning did finally dawn, and with it a new resolve. She would gather the eggs today, no matter how the task frightened her.

James had shown her how to do it once or twice, but she still felt intimidated by the chore. The very idea of reaching under a squawking bird into its warm nest was unnerving, not to mention the possibility of roosters pecking at her shoes and fluttering in her face.

James had chuckled at her timidity, and told her he'd take care of it. But egg gathering was really woman's work, she knew. Besides, he already had enough to do.

She timidly approached the front of the

coop, basket in hand. She had first made certain that the hound, Frank, was nowhere in sight. She wasn't quite so afraid of the dog now, but her heart still skipped a beat when he came galloping up to her. She hoped he was as nice as James said he was, because he had awfully big teeth.

As the sun beat down on her head, Abby decided she had procrastinated long enough. "Well, little one, it's now or never," she said to her unborn child. Flinging open the door of the coop, she hollered, "Rise and shine!"

The startled birds flew everywhere, and Abby backed out of the coop, flailing her arms. "Shoo! Shoo!" she yelled, feeling ridiculous.

"I've never seen it done quite like that before," came an amused voice behind her.

Abby turned with a groan. "Hello, Iris."

James's sister grinned. "What are you doing, Abby?"

"Gathering eggs." She tried to keep a straight face, then gave up. "I thought maybe if I made them all get out first, it might be easier."

"Hmmm." Iris made a comical face, and both women giggled. "Didn't your know-it-all husband show you how to do it?"

"Yes, but I can't stand reaching under

those poor hens." Abby grimaced. "Besides, the smell makes me feel ill."

"You do look a little green, dear," Iris said. "Why don't you go put the teakettle on the stove. I'll gather these eggs."

"You're an angel," Abby said.

Iris snorted. "Don't think I've ever been called that before," she replied. "Here, take this pie into your kitchen. I'll be in before you know it."

Abby headed toward the back door, feeling guilty for allowing her sister-in-law to do her work.

"Hello, girls," she heard Iris say soothingly, and she had to grin. She had never thought of chickens as girls before. She had a lot to learn about farming, that was for sure.

James had been pleased that the eggs were gathered, but Abby felt compelled to admit it was Iris who had done it.

"She's a sweet gal," he said. "She reminds me of my mama."

Abby knew his mother had died in childbirth years ago. "Mothers are very special people," she said softly.

He appeared to be very interested in the piece of pie on his fork, but she could see that his eyes had misted over. "You'll be a wonderful mother, Abby," he whispered.

She stared at him for a moment in silence. Why would he bring that up right now? She cleared her throat. "What kind of pie is this that Iris brought? It's very good."

He speared another bite and took her cue to change the subject. "You've never had rhubarb pie before?"

"Rhubarb?" She poked at the tart red and green chunks that swam in the sweet pink juice, the flaky crust crumbling under her fork. "I've never even heard of it. Perhaps rhubarb doesn't grow in New York."

"Come here and I'll show you." James pushed his chair away from the table and led Abby to a garden patch next to the well. He pointed to a leafy plant growing in the moist, black dirt. Abby had noticed it before, vaguely wondering at its enormous leaves.

"This is a rhubarb plant," he said. "You just reach down and twist on the stalk a little bit." He straightened back up with a slender stalk in his hand. "It's best in the spring."

She smiled up at him, conscious of his nearness as his arm brushed hers. "I think I'll do without the reaching down part for now."

He chuckled, reaching out to pat her stomach. Then apparently catching himself, he jerked his hand away. "Forgive me. I didn't mean —"

"It's all right, James," she said, touching his arm. "After all, you are going to be the child's father." *My goodness!* She hadn't really said that aloud, had she? She had thought of it before, of course, but wouldn't he think that she was being rather presumptuous?

The smile that lit his face was enough to reassure her that she hadn't said the wrong thing. He laid his hand gently on her stomach for a brief moment. "You're right, Abby," he said, his voice husky.

She froze, ensnared by the tenderness that glowed in his sea-blue eyes. What was he thinking?

She didn't have long to wonder. Somehow all of a sudden, she was enfolded in his strong arms. And in that moment, she couldn't think of anywhere else she'd rather be. Couldn't think at all, actually. She just knew that she had come home. She sighed, feeling safe and secure. Loved.

"Uhhh!" The baby kicked. Hard.

James backed away, his eyes wide. Abby had to laugh at the expression on his face, though she wished the moment had not ended so abruptly. "Guess this little one is getting impatient," she murmured, smiling up into James's face.

He grinned. "Me, too."

The look he gave her made her pulse pound and she lowered her gaze to the rhubarb plant. Her commitment to keep her vow was becoming increasingly difficult.

Chapter 5

"Mmm! Something smells good in here!"

"James!" Abby whirled from the stove. "I didn't hear you come in."

He grinned at her and her heart lurched. *He truly is a handsome man,* she thought. *What would it be like — ?*

"Did you fall in?"

"What?" She blinked up at him, feeling flustered.

He chuckled. "Did you fall into the flour bin?"

"Oh." She brushed at her face with her apron, then glanced up to find him directly in front of her. His blue gaze twinkled into hers as his hands gently cupped her face.

"I don't think you got it all off," he whispered, lowering his face to her.

Surely he wasn't going to . . . Her arms slid around him of their own accord, it seemed. He kissed her slowly and tenderly, then pressed her head to his chest. She stood in the circle of his arms, stunned at the feelings coursing through her mind and heart.

Even in her brief marriage to Charles, she had never felt such things. This man seemed to bring out her innate tenderness and vulnerability. Nevertheless, what was she thinking? She would be breaking her promise to God and sinning against Him if she allowed herself to love James Parrish, even if he were her husband.

She pushed her hands against his chest, her heart suddenly leaden. She could not break the vow she had made to God, not even if she wanted to. *And, oh how I want to,* she admitted to herself.

He released her slowly, searching her face as if he sensed the change in her demeanor. "You're precious to me, Abby," he whispered.

She gazed miserably at his beloved face. How could she have possibly thought she could live with such a man and yet not love him?

"Forgive me if I hurt you," he said.

She reached a hand up to his bearded

cheek, loving the feel of the soft bristly whiskers — loving him. "No, I'm the one who's sorry, James." She bowed her head then, ashamed that she should be so weak.

"There's nothing to be sorry for," he told her, trying to draw her back into his arms.

However, she had turned away from him, fussing with the food on the stove.

He kicked at a hay bale that stood next to the barn door, watching as a cloud of dust rose and then settled in the still air. Why had she pulled away from him? She had felt so good in his arms. Just like God made her to fit there. He knew he probably shouldn't have kissed her but, after all, she was his wife!

Dear Lord, surely you haven't brought me this woman just to torture me! I love her, Father. I want her to love me. To want me for her husband. He sighed as he lit the lantern in the chill of the rapidly approaching dusk. What had she meant that day when she said she wasn't a free woman? Would her heart always belong to her first husband, Charles?

Would James have to go on loving her, with no love returned, for the rest of his life? His shoulders drooped at the thought.

How many times had he longed to lay close beside her at night, sharing secrets and feeling their hearts beat as one? Didn't she know that he loved her?

He trudged through the evening chores at a snail's pace, his mind tormenting him with thoughts of what a true marriage could be.

Each passing day brought the birth of Abby's baby ever closer. Since the afternoon that he had kissed her, Abby had withdrawn even more from James. *She is holding up well,* he thought, yet he despaired every time he saw that wounded look in her lovely eyes.

"You look tired," he said one evening, watching as she sank into the rocking chair.

She sent him a weary smile. "It's been a busy day."

Indeed, it had been a busy week. Summer was in full swing, and it seemed every day when he came in for supper, there was another row of canned carrots or tomatoes in the pantry.

"You've been working too hard."

She shrugged. "I want to get as much done as I can before the birth."

She looked more than tired, he observed

as he studied her. Almost haggard. His conscience pricked him. How could he have let her work so hard, especially with the birthing so close? She was probably used to having someone wait on her, he suddenly realized. "Tell me about your life in New York," he said. Maybe if she would at least talk to him, he could understand more of what she was thinking. After all, he really didn't know her.

She looked slightly startled. "What do you want to know?"

I want to know you, his heart cried. "Anything you want to tell me, love," he replied, moving his chair closer.

She stared into the fire. "I grew up there," she began, her voice soft, as if coming from a great distance. "Mama and Papa were so happy together. . . ." She stopped then, as if that was the end of the story.

"Were you happy?" he prompted.

She twisted her hands together, then apparently noticed what she was doing, and held them quietly in her lap. "Yes," she said. "I was happy. I had a wonderful family. I loved God. We went to church."

James nodded, feeling the "but" that must come next.

"Then I met Charles."

The statement dropped into the room like a cold, unexpected shower.

"He convinced me that we should get married." Here she stopped and almost smiled. "So we did. He was a master of persuasion." She glanced at James and shrugged. "Looking back on it now, I'm not sure I ever really loved him. But he convinced me into believing that I did."

James waited, alternating between fear and rejoicing. Fear at what she might say next, yet rejoicing that her heart was not bound to another man.

She shrugged again. "We had only known each other a month before we wed. Papa was livid." She gave James a sad smile. "I was with child soon afterwards. Then . . . a widow."

He grasped her cold hands in his. "What happened, Abby?"

"No one is exactly sure." She grimaced. "I had been over visiting Mama and Aunt Caroline, while Papa went over to our house to talk with Charles about a business matter."

For long minutes the only sound in the room was the crackling of the fire and the squeak of the rocker blades on the smooth floor.

"There was a terrible fire, and Papa and

Charles both died." Her voice was flat, devoid of emotion.

What could he say to her? "I'm s—"

"The constable said that Charles set it on purpose."

"What?" Was she saying what he thought she was?

"Only Charles didn't plan on dying in the blaze, too. He was supposed to live to 'share' in my inheritance."

James felt as if someone had punched him in the gut. No wonder she was reluctant to open her heart to someone again. *But I'm not like that,* he cried silently.

She took a deep breath and gently pulled her hands from his. "So, now you understand why I vowed to God that I would never love again. It was all my fault." She looked away. "I loved Papa and he died. I thought I loved my husband and he turned on me. Now, even Mama . . . she's dying."

How could she think such things were her fault? His heart felt like it was breaking. That phrase had always seemed like a figure of speech to him, until now. What could he possibly say or do to convince her?

Show her the way back to Me, the still, small voice said again.

He bowed his head, surrendering again

to the One who is all-seeing, all-knowing, and never-changing. "Our lives are in Your hands, Father God," he whispered. "Take what we have and who we are, and use us for Your good. We are nothing without You. . . ."

He heard his wife softly weeping and his heart rejoiced to hope that God's spirit was at work in her life.

Hours later, James woke with a start. He could hear Abby thrashing around in the bed, her breaths coming in short gasps. Was it time?

He flew to her side, his own heart pounding. Abby's eyes were squeezed shut, her face contorted with silent terror. A chill traveled down his spine as he felt her fear.

"Jesus!" he prayed aloud, a near frantic urgency in his voice. "Oh, dear Lord, please help my wife. Release her from this consuming fright."

Abby's eyes flew open and James held his breath, watching as the glazed look in her eyes cleared and her rigid body re-laxed. Dropping to his knees, he pressed her limp hand to his face.

"What happened, Abby?" His voice trembled as he spoke.

Abby released a shuddering sigh. "Thank God," she whispered. "It was just another bad dream."

She closed her eyes. "I've had similar nightmares, but . . . but . . ." She opened her eyes to search his face. "This was the worst, by far. Oh, James, I thought I was surely going to die."

He stared at her, his thoughts racing. Apparently she had more to deal with than he had thought. This wasn't simply a woman going through grief. *Father God, please guide my every word,* he prayed. "What was the dream, Abby?"

She shook her head. "I can't. . . ."

"Yes, you can." He tenderly took her chin in his hand. "God doesn't want a child of His to be so tormented by fear."

"Maybe I'm not really God's child."

His heart broke at the bleak words. "Abby, you know God's Word. I've heard you quote the scriptures when I read at night." He smoothed a wispy dark tendril from her forehead. "The Bible says that if you believe in your heart and confess with your mouth that Jesus is Lord, that you are saved."

She nodded. "I've done that. But I don't feel His love, James!" Her voice was pleading. "Why would He make all those terrible things happen to me?"

He took her hand in his. "Abby —"

"I'm so afraid, James! I'm so afraid." Her hand tightened on his. "I just know that something is wrong with my baby. I just know —"

"Hush, now. You mustn't talk like that."

Pursing her lips together tightly, Abby turned her face toward the wall, but not before he caught the glint of betrayal in her eyes.

"Abby, please look at me," he pleaded gently. Minutes ticked by. The darkness in the large room slowly lightened by the break of dawn, yet she remained motionless.

James prayed silently, waiting.

Finally, she turned her eyes to meet his.

"Abby, as God's child, He says to you in Jeremiah 29:11 that He thinks thoughts of peace and not evil toward you. God does not do terrible things to us. Our enemy, Satan, is the one who does that."

She stared at him stonily. "Then why doesn't God stop him?"

"There will come a day when Satan will be bound and rendered helpless. You can be assured of that." He pressed her hand. "But in the meantime, despite life's most dire circumstances, if we saturate ourselves in God's Word, we can experience His peace. Still, a part of the responsibility is ours, too, sweetheart."

She shook her head questioningly. "How is that?"

He smiled, patting Abby's bulging middle lightly. "When our baby is born, he will be hungry. And you will have milk to feed him, right?"

She raised her eyebrows.

"What if this little one chooses not to open his mouth? Will you be able to give him any milk?"

"Of course not. But —"

"You've been doing that to God, Abby. He's waiting for you to accept His peace and His mercy."

She turned her head away again, her long braid sliding over their joined hands. After a long time, her muffled words drew James' attention. "I think He's angry with me."

James gently drew her face toward his. "God is love, Abby. He *is* love."

"But I don't —"

"I know. You've thought and felt and said for so long that God is angry with you and that He doesn't love you — you don't feel or know the truth anymore." He smiled into her eyes, letting all of his love for her show in his face. "You need to start speaking truth and life instead of lies and death. The Word of God says in Proverbs that the power of life and death is in the tongue."

"Oomph!" Abby put a hand over her stomach, her eyes wide. "That was hard!"

James chuckled. "Nothing wrong with that little one."

Abby's dark eyes grew wistful. "I wish I could feel as sure as you do about it."

James ached to kiss away the cares of this woman the Lord had given him, but she needed more than his human love right now. He caressed her face with his eyes. Couldn't she see how much he had grown to love her? He picked up her small hands and placed them on her stomach, chuckling as the child within moved in response.

"My dear," he said, placing his hands on top of hers, "our Heavenly Father is the Creator of all life — including the life of this little one whom we are so anxious to meet. Don't you think that the God who breathes His life in us can be trusted to watch over us all?

"Listen, Abby. The next time you are tempted to allow fear to crowd your thoughts, why don't you pray and ask God to remind you of a Scripture that will replace your fear with His peace."

As the sun rose and the light seeped into the dim room, peace filled Abby's heart for the first time in a very long while.

Chapter 6

"The love of God has been shed abroad in my heart by the Holy Ghost and His love abides in me richly." Abby hummed softly, the words of the scripture from Romans going over and over in her mind like the phonograph records that Mama played. Since James had taught her to use the Scriptures to pray, a whole new spiritual world had unfolded for her.

Abby finished rolling out the piecrust to her satisfaction, then she carefully transferred it to the pie tin. Wouldn't James be surprised to see that she had made him a rhubarb pie? She had gotten the recipe from Iris the last time they had gone to town.

Sinking into a kitchen chair to rest for a

minute before cleaning up the floury mess, she patted the warm lump that rolled underneath her apron. Surely this child would come soon!

A familiar twinge of fear prickled in her heart. "Oh God, don't let —" she started, then stopped, shaking her head. "For God has not given me a spirit of fear, but of power, and love, and a sound mind," she said aloud. "Thank You God. I praise You for Your Word that gives me strength. Your word is a lamp unto my feet and a light unto my path."

She smiled as the child moved again. "I know, little one. I feel His peace, too." Funny how she had known all these Scriptures since she was a small child and yet never realized the power that she possessed as a child of God. It was amazing, really.

She picked up the letters from Mama and Aunt Caroline. James had brought them home from town yesterday, presenting them to her with a smile. "You must be missed," he had said.

Her cheeks grew warm now as she recalled the tender way he had taken her into his arms. It seemed that he had begun to do that more and more often, she mused. Not that she minded, really, but he made it awfully hard to say aloof. Especially when he looked at her with such tender expression in his eyes. She dared not call this feeling "love," but then what else?

She turned back to the letters with a sigh, rereading each one. Apparently, that rascal Aunt Caroline wasn't the least bit repentant of her shenanigans. Abby thought of the elderly woman and smiled. It was so good to hear from her family. Yet, she didn't yearn for home as she expected she would. Had she truly found a home of her own with James?

Her heart warmed as her gaze fell on the cradle. James had brought it home in the back of the wagon, covered carefully with an old quilt.

"I thought we might be needing this soon," he had said, presenting the gift to her almost shyly.

Abby ran her fingertips over the glossy oak. "It's beautiful," she whispered. There were even little heart cutouts in the headboard and a lovely white satin blanket. "You shouldn't have spent so much money," she said, fingering the coverlet.

He chuckled, the sound making her heart sing. "I'm not very good at working with wood, Abby. If I made the cradle, the poor child would probably have fallen through the bottom the first time you laid him in it!"

She laughed, then succumbed to the impulse to run her fingers through his light hair. "I never heard of a farmer who wasn't handy with a hammer," she teased gently.

He smiled down at her, the merriment in his eyes fading into a different emotion. Pulling her to him, he wrapped his arms around her carefully. She leaned against him, reveling in his closeness.

"You must know that I love you, Abby," he whispered into her hair.

She stood still. Did she know that? She thought of him. Thought of all the little things that made up James Parrish. His attentiveness. His gentleness. The way he prayed for her and the baby, his handsome head bowed.

Yes, she knew that he loved her. Even more, she knew that she loved him. And yet, there was the problem. She couldn't love him, or anyone. She had promised.

She sighed now as she dumped the chopped rhubarb into the pastry-lined tin. *It won't help to keep going over and over it,* she told herself sternly. She had made a vow to God, and she intended to keep it.

Abby gathered up the large leaves she had cut off the tops of the rhubarb stalks.

If she chopped them and fried them with a little bacon grease, she could serve the greens with the salt pork and boiled potatoes she was planning for supper. Feeling rather pleased with herself, she got out her sharpest knife.

"I'm as hungry as a bear," James said from outside the back door.

She could hear him scraping the mud off his boots, and smiled. She would have liked to have met his mama, and thanked her for raising such a thoughtful son.

"I'm glad you're hungry, because supper is on the table." She couldn't help smiling at him as he clumped through the door and rewarded her with a kiss on the tip of her nose.

"You're a sight for sore eyes," he said, grinning at her. "When's that baby ever going to come? He should have been here two weeks ago!"

She blew out a good-natured sigh. "You weren't supposed to ask me again, remember?"

He poured water into the basin and plunged his hands into it, scrubbing vigorously. "A man can't help wondering, you know."

Abby smiled behind his back. "I heard

my Aunt Caroline tell many an anxious woman, 'The pear will fall when it's ripe.' "

He laughed aloud. "Sounds like your Aunt Caroline's a pretty wise gal."

"She sent me to you, didn't she?" Abby could have bitten her tongue the minute the words were out of her mouth. Now he would think that she . . . oh dear. There he was looking at her like that again and . . .

The kiss was slow and sweet. Abby thought maybe she had gone to heaven . . . except that there wasn't any smoke in heaven, was there? Smoke? "Oh no! My pie!" She pulled out of his arms and rushed to yank open the oven door.

As she thumped the pie onto the sideboard, relieved to see it still intact, James peered over her shoulder.

"Some of the juice ran over," she mumbled, waving the smoke away with her apron.

James grinned at her sheepishly. "Seems I ought to be praising God for Aunt Caroline."

"What? Oh." She felt her face get red. Was he trying to torment her? She shouldn't have let him kiss her, and he knew it. "Supper's getting cold," she said tartly. She pulled out her own chair without waiting for him and sank into it.

James leaned back in his chair, trying in vain to hold back a snicker. He shouldn't tease Abby so much, he knew, but he couldn't help it. He loved the way she got all flustered and pink-cheeked.

She sent him a mock glare over the table, and he obediently closed his eyes to offer the blessing. He had scarcely said "amen," before she was up and bustling around again.

"Come sit down with me, woman!" he ordered playfully.

She ignored him, busily dipping lemonade into their stoneware mugs. James sighed and turned his attention to the meal. Everything smelled so good. He took an enormous helping of greens, wondering where she had gotten them this time of year. He thought that she had already harvested all the turnips and collard greens.

She dropped heavily into the chair across from him, wiping her forehead with her apron. "Sure is hot for September, isn't it?"

"Mm hmm," he said, his mouth full of potatoes. He took a sip of lemonade. "Fine supper you cooked, Mrs. Parrish."

She grinned at him, the weariness momentarily lifting from her brow. "My mama taught me right, I guess." She watched as he savored a mouthful of greens, her eyes widening when he grimaced.

Good grief! Where did she get these nasty things? It was all he could do not to spit them out on his plate.

"Is something wrong?" Her face was troubled.

He coughed into his napkin, then hastily gulped some lemonade. "Just took a bite of something bitter," he said mildly.

She frowned, tasting a bit from her own plate. Her eyes watered. "You needn't have been so polite, James. They're downright inedible."

He tried not to laugh at the misery on her face. "It's not the end of the world, love. Where did you find these, anyway?"

She made a face. "Well, I wanted to surprise you, so I made a rhubarb pie and — what?"

He closed his eyes briefly, then glanced at her. "Abby, rhubarb leaves are poisonous."

"What? Oh, no, James! I didn't know —"

He reached across the table to capture her shaking hands in his own. "It's all right. Neither one of us ate enough to have any effect."

"How could I have been so stupid?"

His thumbs stroked the backs of her hands soothingly. "I won't tell anyone if you won't."

She sniffed. "I hope you don't think I was trying to k–kill you." A giggle slipped out with the last word, as the humor of the situation struck her. "I can just see the *Denver Post* headlines now: 'New Bride Kills Husband with Mess of Greens.'"

James let loose with the guffaw he had been suppressing. Soon they were howling together, tears streaming down Abby's face. James took a drink, trying to regain a modicum of control, but nearly choked on the liquid when Abby started giggling again.

Finally, they turned their attentions to the cold potatoes and pork, trying not to look at each other, lest they start again. Abby reached for the salt cellar, accidentally bumping James's hand. Their eyes met, which only started James off again with a snort. Abby got tickled all over again, her breath coming in short gasps.

"Stop laughing, James," she said between giggles. "I can't breathe!"

He raised his eyebrows. "Maybe you should take some of these greens to the next church social. Sure would liven things up a bit."

She made a face at him. "You said you wouldn't tell anyone about them."

"Who said I would tell anyone? We could just put them out on the table and let them speak for them — what's wrong?"

She giggled again. "Nothing. I just thought I felt —" Her eyes widened, and she grasped her middle.

James felt his mouth go dry. "Is it time?"

She nodded. "I think so. It must have been those greens."

How could she joke at a time like this? He scraped his chair back and rushed around the table to her. "Shouldn't you lie down?"

She smiled up at him, and his heart turned over. "I think it will be awhile yet, sweet — James." Her face flushed as she caught herself, yet she didn't break eye contact with him.

He stroked her smooth cheek with the back of his fingers. Had she really started to say what he thought she did? Could it be that she was beginning to feel for him even a small bit of what he felt for her? *God, please let it be so!*

"What can I do for you, love?" he whispered. He would never admit this to her, but he was scared stiff at the thought of losing her in childbirth. *God, please help me. . . .*

She leaned her head into his hand. "Just to know that you're here is enough, James."

Abby's predictions proved true. Hours had passed since she felt her first labor pains. James had been almost frantic at first, but he regained his composure as he realized that the birth was not imminent. He had sat next to her throughout the long evening, marveling at the way her stomach would become rock-hard with each contraction. Easy and relatively pain-free at first, they were now becoming harder. More painful. Much more frequent.

"I think it's time to get Ada," Abby murmured.

James stirred from his dozing in the chair next to hers. "What, love?"

"I think you'd better get Ada now," she said, grimacing. *Whew. That one was the hardest yet.*

James clapped his hat on his head, then bent to kiss her tenderly. "Shall I help you into the bed before I go?"

She nodded, fighting back the urge to pant. She didn't want to alarm James, but she was beginning to think that the baby would be here sooner than she had anticipated.

"Hurry, please," she whispered as the door slammed behind him. Why, oh why hadn't she let him fetch the midwife when he wanted to an hour ago? Weeks before, Abby had decided that she'd rather have their neighbor, Ada McReady, as a midwife than a doctor from Denver City. Ada had assured Abby that she had delivered plenty of babies in her fifty years. And it was nice that she lived so close. Abby had met her a time or two in town, and Ada's husband Andy had dropped by with a loaf of her friendship bread when Abby and James had first wed. She was a sweet woman, and at this moment, Abby hoped she was also a speedy woman.

She lay back against the pillow, fighting back the tears. She hadn't realized it would hurt so badly. She tried to pray, but it seemed no words would form in her mind.

She felt like her insides were ripping; the pain and pressure increasing with each contraction. Where were James and Ada?

She felt the familiar blackness of fear beginning to creep at the edges of her mind. What if something was wrong? What if the baby was stuck? What if something happened to her child? All the fear that had been held at bay during the last few weeks of peace came flooding over her.

The pain tore at her, making her cry out. She squeezed her eyes shut tight, trying to think. She should pray . . . she should quote some Scriptures . . . "Jesus!" She screamed the name in prayer, unable to think of anything else.

Immediately the darkness vanished from her mind and calmness descended on her spirit. "Jesus," she whispered. He was there. She could feel the presence of God with her, as strongly as if another human being stood next to her holding her hand. He was God and He loved her. He would not abandon her.

Another wave of pain pulled downward on her body. She gritted her teeth. " 'The Lord is my light and my salvation. Whom . . . shall . . . I . . . fear . . . ?'

" 'He that dwelleth in the secret place of the most High shall . . . abide . . . under the shadow . . . of the Almighty.'

" 'The Lord is . . . my . . . strength . . .' "

She opened her eyes to see James beside her, his strong voice repeating the words with her. He took her hands and held them tightly between his own. "I'm so proud of you," he whispered.

She smiled at him as Ada moved the

quilts to check her. "He heard me, James," she whispered. "Jesus . . . He heard me."

James smiled at her through his tears. "I told you He would," he whispered.

"Well, Mrs. Parrish, I hardly think you needed me," Ada boomed. "You done almost had this babe without me."

Abby squeezed her eyes shut as the searing pain swept through again. "How much . . . longer?" she panted.

"Two or three more good pushes, honey. I can see 'is head already."

James gripped her hands tightly, his eyes never leaving her face. "You can do it, sweetheart," he whispered.

"The Lord . . . is . . . my strength . . . aaagh!" She gave one final push, and it was over.

Seconds later, she felt the hot, wet body of her daughter, lying on her abdomen.

"Hello, little one," she said softly, reaching down to touch her with her fingertips. Her eyes filled with tears when she heard the baby's first quavering wail. "Is she all right, James? Is she truly all right?"

He watched while Ada severed the cord. Then he tenderly wrapped the baby in the soft blanket that awaited. He laid the baby in Abby's waiting arms. "See for yourself, love," he whispered.

And she did see. A beautiful, perfect baby girl. "Thank You, God," she breathed. "Thank You, thank You, thank You!"

She tore her eyes from the child to find James. He had moved across the room and was staring into the fire, his back to her. She frowned. Whatever was he doing way over there? She kissed the baby's soft forehead, and then she knew.

"James, come here please," she called softly. She watched him hesitate, then turn to face her.

She studied his dear face as he came near. Oh, how she loved this man. He had married her, taken her in, provided for her, loved her . . . and what had she given in return? Was he so unsure of her feelings? Did he not know that she wanted him to be a father to her baby — their baby? Could she make him understand?

How she longed to tell him that she loved him — but that was not to be. She choked back the lump that arose in her throat. *God, why did I make such a vow?*

But if she wasn't allowed to give him her heart, at least she could give him this gift. She caressed his face with her eyes as he knelt down by the bed. "James, we need to choose a name for our daughter."

She watched as his eyes, focused on her face, filled with tears. He leaned over to place a tender kiss on her cheek, then bent to kiss the baby's face as well.

"Isn't she beautiful?" Abby murmured.

James nodded, finally finding his voice. "Just like her mama," he whispered.

"Well, it don't look like you folks'll be needin' me anymore." Ada's loud voice made Abby jump. "I'll come check up on y'all tomorrow."

James jumped up to show the midwife out, and Abby turned her attention back to the baby. "Happy birthday, little one," she whispered. She smiled up at James as he neared her side again. "She wants her papa to hold her."

Chapter 7

"Oh, Abby. What a beautiful baby!" Iris held the baby close, her face radiant. "God has truly blessed you!"

Abby smiled. "It's hard to believe she's two weeks old already."

"And I love her name! Anna Joy." Iris kissed the baby's cheek gently. "I'm sorry I couldn't come earlier. I just wanted to make sure . . ."

"Oh, I'm glad you waited," Abby assured her. She would never admit to Iris that every day she had feared a visit from her sister-in-law. Of course, she loved Iris dearly. But, since James had informed her of a smallpox outbreak in town, Abby had feared that little Anna would come down with the dreaded disease.

Even now she cringed inwardly as Iris bent her face near the baby's. What if she was carrying the disease? After all, people were in and out of her boardinghouse every day. She heaved an inward sigh of relief as Iris handed little Anna back to her. The baby gazed into her face, her blue eyes wide and innocent. Abby's arms tightened around her little daughter, her heart overflowing. She was still almost brought to tears each time she considered that this little human being had been entrusted to her care — hers and James's, that is. She glanced over to where he sat at the table, nursing a cup of tea. "Did you tell Iris that I have a new recipe for her to serve at the boardinghouse?"

James grinned at his sister. "Have any guests you'd like to see leave early, Sis?"

"What are you talking about, James?" Iris demanded. "Abby is a wonderful cook!"

"Oh, I agree, Iris." He darted an amused glance at Abby. "She's very frugal, too. After she made a rhubarb pie, she cooked up the leaves for greens."

"Oh no!" Iris gasped. "You didn't!"

Abby laughed. "I'm afraid so. I'm a city girl, remember?"

"Things are never dull around here anymore, that's for sure." James sauntered over to Abby, putting an arm around her shoulders. "God knew what he was doing when He sent me this lady."

Iris chuckled. "I can see that. So — do I get a nephew next time?"

Abby gulped, heat rising to the surface of her cheeks. Iris couldn't possibly know their situation. Undoubtedly James would be too embarrassed to tell his sister. "Well, I —"

"All in good time, Sis. We don't want to rush things when we've only just started to get to know little Anna."

"Well, just don't wait too long." Iris jumped to her feet and smoothed down her skirt in one fluid motion. "Now, I'd best be gettin' back to town. A family's coming in from the Springs tonight." With a quick hug for Abby and a peck on the cheek for James, she was gone.

Abby sank down into the chair with a sigh. "Sometimes just watching Iris makes me tired."

James laughed aloud. "I know what you mean. She's always been a fireball." He crossed over to the cradle, and leaned over to hear Anna's soft breathing. "Think we'll ever take her up on her suggestion?"

Abby wrinkled her forehead. *What was*

he talking . . . ? Oh! How could he so ca-
sually mention that subject when he
knows that I'm bound by my vow to God?
"I don't —"

He lifted his head to look at her then,
and the look in his eyes took her breath
away. "I want us to be a real family, Abby,"
he whispered.

"We are a real —"

"No, we aren't." He crossed over to her
then, standing close enough that she could
feel the heat radiating from his skin. "I
want you for my wife — in every sense of
the word."

She shivered as he ran his hands down
her bare arms. Didn't he know how badly
she wanted that, too? She closed her eyes
against the pleading in his. "Don't you understand, James? I can't!"

He pulled her into his arms almost
roughly. "Abby, you're my wife. I asked
God for a wife and He sent you."

She pushed her face into the strength of
his chest. Confusion flowed through her. If
God had truly sent her to James, then He
expected her to be the best wife she could
be. Certainly God expected one's best. But
then . . . She knew God also required obedience. And if she had made a vow to Him,
she must not break it. Something terrible

would surely happen to James or the baby.

The hopelessness of the dilemma swept over her. She was trapped. Trapped with a loving, desirable man who was her husband — and yet he wasn't. "I don't know what to do," she admitted finally.

His arms tightened around her, and he held her close for a long minute. Then he pulled away enough to look in her eyes. "I promised you that I would always love you and care for you, Abby."

She met his gaze miserably. "I know. And I'm thankful."

His grip tightened slightly. "But that's not enough for me."

She felt a burning shame well up. Was she taking advantage of him? Or was he saying that he now regretted marrying her since she couldn't — or wouldn't — meet his needs?

James watched the emotions play across her face and wondered at her thoughts. He was pretty sure by now that she felt at least a bit of love for him. Why couldn't she take that final step and admit it? Oh, he knew full-well of her vow. But he had assumed that, by now, she would have realized her flawed logic. He had thought that, perhaps after the baby was born . . . He heaved a great sigh and dropped his hands from her shoulders. "Guess I'll tend to the chores."

The evenings were turning chilly now, he thought vaguely as he trudged toward the barn. He glanced back at the house, watching through the lighted window as Abby knelt to pick up little Anna. A lump rose in his throat, and he turned his eyes back to the well-worn path. "God, surely You don't require her to honor a vow that she made in ignorance," he cried aloud.

Only the lonely cooing of the doves answered him in the still night air.

After several days of strained conversation between them, James longed to return to their easy camaraderie. Perhaps he had been too impatient. Maybe he had just pushed her too hard when she wasn't ready. They could use a good laugh together, he decided. He pushed open the back door, surprised to find the house dark and cold. Why hadn't she lit the lamps?

"Boy, I'm hungry for some greens tonight," he joked as he removed his hat.

Abby barely spared him a glance, her face anguished as she rocked Anna in the dim light.

James felt his heart contract. "What's wrong, Abby?" he whispered, coming to stand in front of her.

"I knew it. I just knew this would happen," she moaned.

He wasn't sure she was even aware of his presence. He stopped the monotonous motion of the rocker with his foot. "Abby!" he said, concern ringing in his voice. "What is it?"

She lifted her eyes to his, and his heart went cold. *Father God, please help me,* he prayed silently. He knelt down in front of her. "Abby. Tell me what's wrong."

She shook her head. "I knew it would happen. He doesn't love me, James. You said He did, but He doesn't."

"Abby." James took a deep breath. "Please stop talking nonsense. And tell me what has upset you."

Her body hunched over the baby. Her shoulders heaved with wrenching sobs. "Oh, James. She's sick, James. Our little Anna is sick. I just know she's going to die!"

He wrapped his arms around her. *God, help us,* he pleaded silently.

Tenderly, James lifted the infant from Abby's lap and into his arms. "Oh, dear God." The unchecked prayer slipped from his lips when he saw the blister-like spots that covered the soft, pale skin. "Dear God."

Hugging the baby to his chest, he let the tears fall. Yet, even as he held the child in his arms, his heart was filled with a sense of peace. He pressed a kiss onto the small forehead and drew a deep breath. "I can't put my feelings into words, Abby. But I feel confident that our baby won't die."

Abby shrugged her shoulders. "God allowed her to get sick. Why wouldn't He let her die?"

"I can't promise you that He won't, Abby, but I trust Him to do what is best for Anna and for us. He clutched the baby's feverish body closer to him. "We must trust Him with Anna. He loves her even more than you do."

"Don't you see? Tragedy just seems to follow me —"

"No," he said gently. "I don't see. Trials and tests and tribulations come to us all, Abby. Not just to you." He laid a comforting hand on her cheek. "God will give us the strength to face even this."

He handed the baby back to Abby, then strode over toward the fireplace. He stirred up the fire and threw another log on. After lighting the lamps, he shrugged into his coat and jammed his hat on his head. "I'm going to fetch Ada. She's as good as any doctor in these parts. Besides, she's a woman of deep faith and she can help us pray." James paused at the door, his hand gripping the knob. He turned to watch his wife. She sat in silence, blinking at the light. "I'll hurry back as quickly as I can, but don't just sit there and cry while I'm gone. Pray."

The door slammed behind him. Abby leaned her head back in the rocker and closed her eyes. *Pray? My prayers won't help. I've prayed and prayed in the past. Has God ever answered my prayers?*

Anna whimpered, and Abby automatically held her closer, adjusting her blankets. It had been hours since the babe had nursed. Abby's breasts felt achingly full, yet the baby refused to eat. "Come on, little one," she coaxed. "You need to eat." The child sucked weakly for a moment, then turned her head away. Her little mouth clamped closed.

Abby sighed and her tears threatened to overflow. The child wouldn't have enough strength to get well if she didn't eat soon. Abby slowly buttoned her bodice, suddenly recalling James' words of a few months ago. "Part of the responsibility is ours, love," he had said. "Just as you can't feed a baby who refuses to open its mouth, you limit God by refusing to accept His ways and His comfort."

Was she really doing that, she wondered? Could it be that God had really been there through her whole life, and she had refused to accept Him, the very One who would strengthen her?

It seemed that she had begun to learn His ways just before Anna was born, but somehow, she had fallen and slipped back. She could see that clearly now as she looked back on the last few weeks.

She had slipped out of the habit of reading God's Word daily and had stopped praying so much when Anna arrived healthy and happy. How could she have done that? How could she have forgotten the way His presence comforted her during the birthing? "Oh God, forgive me," she cried inwardly. Was He angry with her? Was that why her baby was sick?

A few months ago she would have assumed this to be true, but now . . . she wrinkled her brow as she struggled to recall the verses James had shown her. Wasn't there one that said something about there being no condemnation for those who were in Christ Jesus? Yes, she was sure of it. James had explained that that verse meant that once she had confessed her sin and asked God to forgive her, He would. He wouldn't be angry with her. She sighed in relief.

" 'Why so downcast, oh my soul? Put your hope in God!' " The verse from Psalms popped into her mind with such clarity that she was startled. Could she really put her hope in God at a time like this?

She sat up straighter, feeling determination flood through her. "I will." She said the words aloud. "I choose to trust God this time."

Hoisting herself out of the rocking chair, she carried the whimpering baby over to the window. Gazing out into the star-filled night, she felt her heart stir within her. If God, who created all things, could love her, then she surely could trust Him.

Abby tenderly placed Anna into her cradle in hopes that the baby would rest. As she eased back into her rocking chair beside the cradle the door flew open. James strode inside, followed by Ada. The neighbor scurried to the baby's cradle and began examining her with a physician's skill. James came up beside Abby and put his arm around her. "Don't be afraid," he whispered in her ear. She laid her head against his shoulder.

"I'm not," she whispered, marveling at the thought. "I'm not afraid."

As Ada worked over the child, rubbing a concoction of Croton Oil and Tartaremetic Ointment into the tiny chest, James began to sing a familiar hymn. Abby closed her eyes, joining her voice with his. The presence of God filled the room in a way that Abby had never experienced before. She opened her eyes, almost expecting to see Him standing beside her. When their song ended and Ada finished her nursing tasks, an expectant hush filled the room. James gently lifted the baby from the cradle, his hands trembling. The trio of adults huddled around the child, and Abby sensed God's presence encircling them as James began to pray.

"Father God, we bring little Anna to You." His voice broke. "God, we dedicated her to You when she was born. She belongs to You, not us. But God, we love her, and we know that You have the power to heal her." He dipped his finger into a jar of oil that Ada had retrieved from her bag of medicines and doctoring supplies.

"Father God, in Your Word, You teach us, if there are any sick among us, that we are to anoint them with oil and they will be healed."

Ada placed a gentle hand on the baby's chest and added her voice to James's prayer. "Dear Lord, on behalf of this precious little child, Anna, we pray that You will touch her body and spare her life."

Abby wanted to join James and Ada in their spoken prayers, but she was too choked with emotion to vocalize her petition. The words refused to leave her lips. She silently pleaded with the Lord, adding an emotional "Amen" to the others' prayers.

She felt her heart constrict as James rubbed a drop of oil onto Anna's forehead. Something gave way inside Abby at that moment. She couldn't hold back the tears as she realized, clearly and finally, that God loved Anna — and God loved her. He wanted them both to be well and whole. Although she couldn't fully fathom the thought, she suddenly understood that God loved her much more than she loved her own baby. She, Abby Parrish, was His child, just as Anna was her child. It was as if she had never understood that before.

She reached over and took the baby from James, her heart rejoicing in fresh revelation. God Almighty loved her!

Anna's sudden loud cry took Abby by surprise, and she smiled up at James when he chuckled. "I think she's hungry," she said in amazement.

He nodded, placing a large hand on the child's head. "I believe the fever's gone."

Abby pressed her cheek to Anna's face. It was smooth and cool. She felt fresh, happy tears streaming down her cheeks once more, but she let them fall freely. "Thank You, God," she whispered.

The next few weeks were filled with wonder and joy, as Abby marveled constantly over God's love for her and His healing of Anna. Finally she felt as if her heart was beginning to understand what God's Word said.

"It's like I see things so much clearer now," she said to Iris one day.

The older woman bounced Anna on her lap. "That's what happens when we open ourselves up to the Holy Spirit and let God teach us through His Word."

"For the first time, I feel like I really know God loves me."

"And your husband does, too."

Abby jumped. "James, I didn't hear you come in." Her face burning, she refused to look at Iris. Was he trying to embarrass her?

Iris handed the baby to him. "This little girl wants her daddy, and Aunt Iris needs to get back to town." She bent to hug Abby and whispered in her ear. "Don't deny yourself your husband's love, Abby."

Abby clenched her jaw. How could Iris know anything of her feelings? How could she know the many nights Abby had lain in bed, exhausted, yet sleep would not come? How could she know the anguish of love that could never be fulfilled?

Iris straightened up and patted her shoulder. "Bring that little one for a visit soon," she said, her bright tone belying the meaningful look in her eyes as Abby finally met her gaze.

Abby nodded shortly, then blew out a sigh as the door swung shut behind her sister-in-law.

"What was that all about?" James's handsome face wore a frown.

Abby shrugged. What could she tell him? That she was ashamed because his sister had guessed the truth about their marriage? Or that even though she was now assured of God's love for her, she could never give her husband that same assurance of her love? Perhaps she should just go ahead and tell him of her love and disregard her vow to God. Yet, the very thought made her shudder. Surely she owed God even more, now that He had healed little Anna.

"Abby?" *What is going on in her mind?*

"I . . . I'm sorry, James." She gave him a wan smile. "Guess I lost my train of thought."

He fought against a twinge of rising irritation. For days now, he had watched as she fluctuated between joy and despair. "Abby, if you're worried that I'm going to force myself on you now that you're no longer with child —"

"Oh no!" She looked shocked. "I never thought that."

Well, that's good, at least, he thought grimly. *Or is it?* Didn't she know how much he desired her as his wife? He had tried to be kind and very patient. But things didn't appear to be changing any time soon. He had prayed the best he knew how. Quite frankly, his hope was waning. How long must his heart wait to hear her utter sweet words of love? His frustrated thoughts found their way into words before he had time to consider the consequences.

"Abby, I don't know what more I can do to win your love. Won't you ever love me — like I love you? Must you cling to that absurd vow of yours forever?"

Her face flushed, and he could have kicked himself for airing his regrets and disappointments so. Why had he so frankly exposed his feelings? Surely such bluntness would only hinder his cause, not help.

"I'm sorry," she said again. Her voice was quiet, filled with resignation.

So this was the way it was going to be. He placed the infant in her cradle, then turned abruptly toward the door. "I'm sorry, too, Abby. More than you could know."

The door banged shut, punctuating his words with finality. Abby stared after him, despair threatening to overwhelm her. "God, what else can I do? I promised You. And I have to keep my vow, don't I? I promised that I would never give another man my heart. And now that I know how much You love me, how could I even think about breaking my vow?"

She buried her face in her hands. What had she done? *I never should have married you, James,* she thought in agony. *You're too good of a man to be stuck with me.*

The baby whimpered, and Abby tended to her automatically. "Mama loves you," she whispered through her tears. "Mama won't ever leave you, little one," she crooned.

God had saved her baby's life, and she

owed Him a great debt, of that she was sure. Now she felt it was even more imperative that she keep her vow. Maybe she should do James a favor and leave. Then he would be free to find someone who could be the true wife he deserved.

The following days were agony as a heavy silence settled between them. James spoke to her only when necessary, his mouth held in a grim line the rest of the time. He had moved out to the barn, for all practical purposes, even sleeping in one of the empty stalls.

Does he despise me so much that he can't even sleep in the same house? Abby wondered. She felt at an impasse, unable to find a solution. They couldn't go on like this much longer — and surely not for the rest of their lives.

"I should never have married you, James," she said softly one night.

He whirled around, his blue eyes filled with pain. "Please, don't utter such words ever again. I love you dearly, Abby. God answered my heart's prayer when He brought you into my life. No matter how you feel about me, I love you. You are my wife and I am totally committed to you." His voice broke on the last words, and he turned away from her again.

She was powerless to resist the urge to wrap her arms around him. It was the first time she had dared touch him in days. With the gesture of affection, the floodgates of her soul opened. She laid her head against his strong back, feeling him stiffen at her touch. Then turning in her arms, he gathered her against him. He buried his face in her neck, and she felt his hot tears mingling with her own.

"I don't know what to do, James," she sobbed. "I don't know what to do."

He held her as if he would never let go. "Hush, now. We'll figure out the rest later." His arm tightened around her, protecting her, shielding her, giving her hope. Could there possibly be a way to have her husband's love and God's approval at the same time? She felt almost traitorous in thinking it.

She pulled away from him, searching his face as if she could will him to know how much she loved him.

He took a deep breath. "I'm sorry for my behavior of late, Abby." He cupped her cheek in his large, work-roughened hand. "I just love you so much, and I don't understand why we —"

"But you know why, James," she burst

out in frustration. Why did he have to make it worse?

"No, I don't know why. If it's because you made some sort of promise to God out of ignorance —"

"It doesn't matter." She stepped back from him, as if putting physical distance between them would help her get ahold of her thoughts. "It doesn't matter. I made the vow, and I have to keep it."

"I don't believe that, Abby."

"What?" She stared at him as if he had lost his senses. "Doesn't God require obedience?"

He ran his fingers through his hair. "Yes. Yes, of course He does. But I don't think that's what we're talking about here."

She frowned. What was he getting at?

"I think that out of your pain and confusion, you tried to make a bargain with God."

She had never looked at it that way before. "But I still promised."

He sighed. "I know." He looked like he wanted to shake her. "But don't you understand? God brought us together, Abby. He has blessed you with a future and a hope."

She shook her head. It couldn't be that easy. She couldn't simply sit back and take what He had handed her, even if it was something good.

"God loves you," James said, as if reading her thoughts. "He sent Jesus to die, to forgive our sins, but also to give us life, and even abundant life, the Bible says."

Could that really be true? She pressed her hand to her forehead. "I'm just so confused."

"God is not a God of confusion, Abby." James reached for his Bible. "It says in here that God does not give us a spirit of fear, but of power and love and a sound mind."

"But —"

"Do you think being fearful and worried about this is what God wants for you?"

She shrugged. "But I don't deserve —"

"Deserve?" James interrupted. "Why, Abby, none of us deserves a single one of God's gracious gifts. We don't deserve them, nor can we earn them." He smiled. "I knew there was something that was keeping you from understanding this." He pulled his Bible from the table and intently flipped through the pages until he came to the verse he had been seeking. "Here, read it for yourself. The second chapter of Ephesians, verse eight. Do you see it?"

She looked where his finger jabbed the

page. "For by grace are ye saved through faith; and that not of yourselves: it is the gift of God: Not of works, lest any man should boast." She read it again, aloud this time. Before she could say anything, he was flipping pages again.

"Now, read this one," he pleaded.

"For . . . ye have been called unto liberty; only use not liberty for an occasion to the flesh, but by love serve one another." She squinted up at him. "What does this mean?" she whispered. Surely it didn't mean what she suspected.

James framed her face with his hands. "It means," he said, "that you are free. It means that we obey God out of love and gratefulness, not out of duty, debt . . . or fear."

She was speechless.

James put the Bible down and drew her into his arms gently. "Father God, please reveal Your love to Abby. Open her eyes of understanding. She is not to serve You out of anything but love and gratefulness. Nor for anything she needs to repay, and not because of anything she has done or not done. She is Your child because she accepted Your Son. And she is righteous in Him alone."

Abby lay in bed, her mind racing. Could

it really be as simple as James made it sound? That she didn't have to work and strive to pay her debts to God?

She closed her eyes, hearing the chilly fall wind howling past her window. She shivered, pulling the quilt up tighter under her chin. In the faint light of the banked fire, she could see James sleeping in front of the hearth. *Dear James.* She smiled, glad that he had moved back in the house from the barn. She pictured him lying next to her, his arms holding her close.

Her cheeks burned guiltily at the thought. Surely God would be displeased with her if she broke her vow, and something bad would happen. It just couldn't be as easy as James had made it sound.

She heard Frank whimper outside the door, and she groaned. That dog never could stand to be outside when a storm was brewing. And from the sound of that wind, they were in for some snow tonight.

She crawled out of bed, shivering as her bare feet touched the icy wood floor. She must be crazy, getting up to let a dog in the house. Somehow the big creature had grown on her, she supposed. She'd better make sure the baby was warm enough, too. They were overdue for the first snowstorm of the season.

Frank scratched at the door again. "I'm coming," she murmured. Glancing out the window as she made her way to the cradle, her heart stopped.

Surely she was imagining it — no! There was another flicker — "James!"

He woke with a start.

"James! The barn is on fire!"

"What?" He pulled his trousers on over his long johns. "Get some water and prime the pump," he yelled over his shoulder as he flew out the door.

Her hands shaking, she grabbed the tin bucket, full of water, from its place beside the door. Closing the door softly behind her so she wouldn't awaken Anna, she stepped into the chill of the night. She ran toward the pump, refusing to think of what would happen if the fire reached the house.

Images of her home in New York, charred beyond recognition, flashed into her mind. She could imagine Papa's anguished cries for help, could smell the burning flesh — "Jesus!" she cried aloud. "Please help us!" She tripped over Frank and went sprawling, but somehow she managed to keep most of the water from spilling. She clambered back to her feet, hot tears streaming down her face. *Fear not, for I am with thee*. The bit of

Scripture floated into her mind. *Fear not. Fear not.*

She reached the pump, feeling for the handle in the dark. Her breath came in short gasps, whether it was from exertion or fear she wasn't sure. The water began to flow, and as it did, she felt God's presence flow over her once again like the day He had healed Anna.

I will never leave you or forsake you, Abby. The Spirit's gentle voice broke into her consciousness.

James stumbled up with two buckets. "Keep pumping, Abby!" he shouted.

She obeyed, listening as the water gushed out to fill the pails. "I love you, James," she said suddenly.

For a long moment, James stood motionless. "What did you say?"

"I said I love you and I want to be your wife."

"Hallelujah!" He dropped the buckets and swung her into his arms.

"James, the barn!" she murmured against his lips.

He set her down reluctantly and grabbed the buckets. "God will see us through, Abby," he said.

And so He did. The fire somehow stayed

contained in the tack room, destroying everything in there, but not moving beyond to the stalls. "It's a miracle," James said the next morning, as they stood gazing at the soot-covered room. Snow had fallen lightly, making the scene seem cold and unreal.

Abby nodded, her heart too full for words. The night had certainly been one to remember. After the fire was finally out, she and James had collapsed onto the rockers in front of the fireplace.

"Thank God you saw the sparks in time, Abby," James had said, his voice hoarse from the smoke.

She nodded. "I got up to let Frank in and glanced out the window."

He ran a hand through his hair, leaving it standing on end. "We didn't lose any of the animals. That's the most important thing." He stared at the fireplace, as if lost in thought.

Abby felt her stomach clench. Was he thinking the same thing she was? How could she have blurted that out, there by the pump? It wasn't as if anything had changed, really. . . .

"Did you mean what you said out there, Abby?"

She felt the blood rise to her face, but

she couldn't ignore the look in his eyes as he turned to gaze at her. "I . . ." She saw the uncertainty flicker across his dear face. "Yes."

He slid down to his knees in front of her, laying his head in her lap. "You don't know how I've longed to hear you say those words."

She tangled her fingers in his blond hair. "I've wanted to say them for a long time," she confessed. "I do love you, James."

He raised his head. "What changed, my dear one?" he whispered.

How could she explain it? She shrugged. "I guess I . . . finally figured out that God is on my side. He is not hovering over me, just looking for ways to hurt me."

James nodded. "He is Love."

"Yes." She put a hand to his reddened cheek. "And so, last night, I felt that God wanted me to make another vow. A vow I am more committed than ever to keeping."

He looked stunned. "What do you mean, Abby?" His voice was strained and his eyes pleaded with her. "What are you saying? I thought you . . ."

"No, wait." She grasped his hands. "Let me tell you what I promised God. I vowed to love the Lord my God with all my strength, my soul, my mind, and my spirit.

I intend to keep my vow and to never love another like I should love Him alone."

James gripped her shoulders. "Is there room in there somewhere for me?"

She moved into his embrace, her heart overflowing. "Always," she whispered. "I promise."

Epilogue

"It's a boy!" James's joyful shout was music to Abby's ears. Could it be possible that almost a year had gone by since the night of the barn fire? That night was forever imprinted on Abby's memory. It was a night of endings, as well as sweet beginnings. The ending of fear and bondage. The beginning of life and love.

"I told you I wanted a nephew. Now, here he is," Iris sang out joyfully from beside the bed. "God has blessed you again, Abby."

Abby looked up to find her husband's tender gaze fixed on her face.

"Thank you," he whispered. "You've given us another beautiful child."

Her eyes filled with tears. How had God

taken a bitter vow and turned it into an unending promise of joy? She held out her arms for her new little son, then clasped James's hand. She kissed Anna's little forehead as she snuggled up close. "Mama and Papa will love you both forever," she vowed softly. And she smiled, knowing this was a vow that would remain forever unbroken.